ESER T

CARTOGRAPHER'S
• HILL

fallingstar
road

SHWORKS

thered funicula

pokenose
peak

Pfefferminz Ridge

ines of
rrow

CURSEWORKS

• realm of the
spider lords

• SQORPIUS
HARBOR

RECHAUN
UNTY ☘

.ooplewhoop's
erlasting
rcus

• shaleleigh

N

W          E

S

The Misadventures of
# Benjamin Bartholomew Piff

# **2** *Wishful Thinking*

Written and illustrated by
Jason Lethcoe

Grosset & Dunlap

*Cover illustration by Katrina Damkoehler*

GROSSET & DUNLAP
Published by the Penguin Group
Penguin Group (USA) Inc., 375 Hudson Street, New York, New York 10014, U.S.A.
Penguin Group (Canada), 90 Eglinton Avenue East, Suite 700, Toronto, Ontario,
Canada M4P 2Y3 (a division of Pearson Penguin Canada Inc.)
Penguin Books Ltd, 80 Strand, London WC2R 0RL, England
Penguin Ireland, 25 St Stephen's Green, Dublin 2, Ireland
(a division of Penguin Books Ltd)
Penguin Group (Australia), 250 Camberwell Road, Camberwell, Victoria 3124, Australia
(a division of Pearson Australia Group Pty Ltd)
Penguin Books India Pvt Ltd, 11 Community Centre, Panchsheel Park, New Delhi—110 017,
India
Penguin Group (NZ), 67 Apollo Drive, Rosedale, North Shore 0745, Auckland, New Zealand
(a division of Pearson New Zealand Ltd)
Penguin Books (South Africa) (Pty) Ltd, 24 Sturdee Avenue, Rosebank, Johannesburg 2196,
South Africa

Penguin Books Ltd, Registered Offices:
80 Strand, London WC2R 0RL, England

Text and interior illustrations copyright © 2007 by Jason Lethcoe. Cover illustration copyright
© 2007 by Katrina Damkoehler. All rights reserved. Published by Grosset & Dunlap, a division
of Penguin Young Readers Group, 345 Hudson Street, New York, New York 10014. GROSSET &
DUNLAP is a trademark of Penguin Group (USA) Inc. Printed in the U.S.A.

Library of Congress Control Number: 2007000464

ISBN 978-0-448-44497-0                    10 9 8 7 6 5 4 3 2 1

*For my mom, who taught me how to wish.*

*Hope Springs Eternal*

# TABLE OF CONTENTS

# CHAPTER ONE
## Ben's Surprise

"**A** Flooper Fizz and a basket of fish-and-chips, please." Benjamin Bartholomew Piff watched as the surly leprechaun spooned some glittering syrup onto the wooden tray he was carrying. Seconds later the magical syrup transformed into a glass of Ben's favorite drink and a basket of crispy fish and fries.

"Thanks," Ben said, reaching for a fry.

"Keep the line moving," the leprechaun said, waving his big spoon.

Ben walked to the side and scanned the packed Pot o'

Gold restaurant for his friends Jonathan, Gene, Nora, and Fizzle. He couldn't wait to tell them his big secret.

Even though it was a bright, beautiful June afternoon, the inside of the Pot o' Gold looked like twilight. The light was dim, and glowing paper lanterns were suspended in the pine trees that surrounded the grassy eating area.[1] Ben always found the restaurant a welcome break from his busy job as manager of Kids' Birthday Wishes Ages 3 to 12.

It was hard for Ben to believe that just six months earlier he had been a miserable orphan at Pinch's Home for Wayward Boys. His life had changed after he'd made a wish for unlimited wishes on his eleventh birthday. The resulting wish had nearly destroyed the Wishworks Factory and given Curseworks, Wishworks's oldest rival, an opportunity to torment the whole world with horrible, living curses.

Ben thought about the dangerous mission he had undergone to steal the globe that contained his powerful wish from the hands of evil Curseworks president Adolfus Thornblood and shuddered. If it hadn't been for Thomas Candlewick, the president of Wishworks and Ben's mentor,

---

[1] The Pot O' Gold was commissioned by Patrick McMurphy, the very first leprechaun president that the Wishworks Factory ever had, in 1745. The atmosphere in the themed restaurant is so dark because leprechaun magic is at its most powerful during sunrise and sunset.

he might not have made it out of Curseworks alive!

It was shortly after his daring rescue that Candlewick had offered Ben his job. It was the happiest day of Ben's life. Living at the Wishworks Factory was the closest thing Ben had had to a real home since his parents had died a year and a half earlier.

"Hey, Ben! Over here!" someone suddenly called out.

Ben looked toward the huge tree-stump tables. There was Jonathan Pickles, motioning for him to come over. Ben grinned and pushed the brim of his oversize top hat away from his eyes, then crossed the field of clover to his waiting friends.

"Hi, guys!" Ben said. As he sat down at the big stump he noticed that someone was missing. "Where's Fizzle?"

Nora, a cute leprechaun with mousy brown hair and almond-shaped eyes, answered.

"Her grandpa isn't doing well. She left this morning to go visit him at his Gum Shop[2]." She took a bite of a raspberry scone that was as big as her head.

---

[2] Fizzypop's Gum Shop in the Land of Faerie is said to carry over 1400 magical varieties of gum. They range from chewable cures for common maladies, such as seasickness or the common cold, to incredible flavors that can temporarily make the chewer invisible, change into strange creatures, or sprout incredibly long, noodlelike nose hairs. The last flavor mentioned is seldom used, except by people desperate to make an impression at a party or social gathering, usually with disastrous results.

"I hope he's going to be okay," Ben said, concerned for his little fairy friend.

"She promised to let us know how he's doing," Gene put in quickly.

As he set his tray down on the big stump's smooth surface, Ben noticed that someone had carved his or her initials into the tabletop with a pocketknife. The letters *T.C. +D.N.* stood out boldly, surrounded by a crudely carved heart. Annoyed, Ben moved his tray to cover the graffiti. He didn't like when people disrespected his favorite restaurant.

"So, what's this big secret you have?" Nora asked eagerly.

"Yeah, this better be good," Jonathan added. "When you called, I was in the middle of fixing a loose gear on the Thaumaturgic Cardioscope's earpiece."

Ben knew that Jonathan had made a big sacrifice by taking a break to meet him for lunch. In the six months since they had started at the Factory as interns, Ben and his friends had all found entry-level jobs. Jonathan worked in a cupcake-shaped building that had a giant brass ear sticking out of the top. Even though the building was funny-looking on the outside, serious business went on inside. The building possessed intricate machinery capable of listening in on the heartfelt wishes of children all over the world. If not for the maintenance supplied by its dedicated technicians like Jonathan, the Thaumaturgic Cardioscope wouldn't be able to keep its twenty-four-hour-a-day schedule.[3]

"Look!" Ben blurted out. "When I got up this morning, *this* was in my mailbox." He pushed up the sleeve of his brown jacket to reveal an unusual gold watch.

Gene looked at his wrist with a quizzical expression. "A watch? *That's* the big surprise?" Ben couldn't help but notice that his purple Jinn friend looked slightly disappointed.

Jonathan grabbed Ben's wrist and leaned over to examine the watch more closely.

"No way." He whistled lightly through his teeth. "Where did you get *that*?"

"It's from Thom." Ben's mentor had his own magical gold pocket watch that could transport him anywhere in the world with a press of a button. He had told Ben that when Ben was ready to take on the full-time role of manager, he would be given a watch. Ben could hardly believe that it had finally happened!

---

[3] The Thaumaturgic Cardioscope failed only once in Wishworks Factory history. This happened when a new employee on the night shift accidentally fell asleep and forgot to wind the machine's massive clockwork. The resulting disaster was the Stock Market Crash of 1929. Since that time, an alarm system has been installed that routinely wakes up drowsy employees working the graveyard shift.

"That's cool, but what does it mean?" Gene asked.

"It means that I'm going on my first solo mission!" Ben's eyes danced with excitement. "Finally! No more riding shotgun with Thom."

Up until now, Ben had always watched carefully from a distance while Thomas Candlewick had delivered birthday wishes. Ben had learned a lot from watching a master at work. Candlewick effortlessly navigated the difficult questions that usually arose from confused parents who couldn't understand where the fulfilled wish had come from. This was especially difficult when he delivered impossible items like full-size airplanes, circus elephants, or chests of pirate gold.

Nora admired the watch's tiny hands, which were shaped like lit birthday candles. The tips of the little glowing flames pointed to miniature birthday cakes instead of numbers, and a counter on the face listed the number of children's birthday celebrations on that day.

"It's one of my dad's." Nora glanced up at Ben. "You can tell because he put his initials near the bottom, see?"

Ben looked down at the watch face where Nora indicated. The initials *S.O.* were printed in tiny letters near the sixth birthday cake.

"Your dad made this?"

Nora nodded proudly. "Yep, we O'Doyles have made

watches for Wishworks since the very first president of the Factory. My mum and dad run the shop down in Leprechaun County[4]."

"Wow," Ben said admiringly.

Nora grinned. "You'd like it there. They're always inventing new magical stuff to put in their watches. They wanted me to work in the shop, but I had a different career path in mind." Nora looked up at Ben with a secretive expression. "By the way, do you know anything about your first mission?"

Ben took a sip of Flooper Fizz. "Not sure. But I heard that a kid wished for a working steam locomotive this morning." He glanced at Nora, who still had a mysterious look on her face. "Why, do you know something that I don't?"

Nora shrugged. "Not telling. You'll have to wait and find out."

"Man, I would love to have a watch like that," Jonathan

---

[4] O'Doyle's Timepieces is currently owned by Seamus O'Doyle, who inherited it from his great-grandfather Nulty. The magical watches are so intricate that they sometimes take up to two hundred years to create. Consequently, most Wishworks presidents order them for their great-grandchildren far in advance. In Ben's case, the watch that he currently owns was supposed to be a gift from Penelope Thicklepick to her nephew Bert. Bert died before he could inherit the watch and Candlewick was able to purchase it at a reduced rate.

interrupted. "I would zap myself over to Chesterton's Cogs[5] and get all the stuff I needed without having to waste my time flying by Feathered Funicula all the way over there and back."

"Whaddya mean, *wasting* time flying by Feathered Funicula?" Gene challenged, puffing out his chest and pretending to be offended. Ben knew that there was nothing Gene loved more than piloting the incredible winged chairs that the Factory workers used to get from place to place.

Since the war with Curseworks, Ben had heard Candlewick remark that Gene was being closely watched by some of the Factory's most experienced Feathered Funicula pilots. The sixteen-year-old Jinn was the youngest pilot ever accepted into the prestigious Four Leaf Clover Squadron.

Ben chuckled. "Hey, by the way, how's it going with the Squadron training?"

Gene shrugged his massive shoulders and sighed.

"Tyrone Crunchapple's a tough instructor. He didn't

---

[5] "If you need it, we probably don't have it" is the advertising slogan of Chesterton's Cogs and Clockworks. It has proven to be one of the most inventive campaigns ever designed, for in spite of its negative implications, most people refuse to believe that the shop had them specifically in mind when they came up with the slogan. Oddly enough, business for Chesterton Cogs is booming even though they really don't carry anything the shopper actually needs.

even blink when I did a triple barrel roll yesterday[6]."

"Wow. You really did a triple?" Ben was impressed. "If I ever tried that, I think I would lose my lunch!"

Jonathan elbowed the Jinn boy in the ribs. "I saw ol' Purple Butt out there yesterday doing loop-de-loops and stalls, showing off for a group of Jinns outside the Cardioscope." He chuckled. "You should have seen Crunchapple. He was so mad, he almost pulled out the rest of his green hair trying to get Gene to stop hotdogging!"

Gene grabbed a handful of fries and playfully tossed them at Jonathan's head. "Yeah, well, it was worth it. I impressed one of the girls, Jeannie. We're going to the Wing and a Prayer Café for lunch on Saturday."

"Wait, you don't mean Jeannie our friend, right?" Ben asked, confused.

He still couldn't get used to the Jinn practice of never revealing their real names to anybody but their most intimate family. All Jinn boys were called Gene and the girls Jeannie by non-Jinns.

"Of course not," Nora said with a laugh. "He wouldn't

---

[6] Only two other pilots in the Wishworks Factory history, Charles Featherflip in 1927 and Beatrice Rhinnynose in 1945, attempted the triple barrel roll. Both pilots made two and a half rotations before falling out of the cockpit and landing unceremoniously in a nearby lake.

date his *sister!*"

Ben stared at Gene, surprised. "Jeannie's your sister? How come you never told me?"

"You never asked," Gene said, his mouth full of French fries.

Ben held out his hands in a helpless gesture. "I had no idea! Besides, the whole name thing is confusing. The other day I mentioned you to some guys at the Fulfillment department and it took me half an hour of describing what you looked like before they knew which Gene I was talking about." Ben took a bite of fish before continuing. "It would be a whole lot easier for all of us if you could just tell us your real name. After all, we *are* your best friends."

Gene folded his massive arms across his chest and sighed. "You guys know I can't. No offense, but my dad would kill me if I ever did that."

Ben knew that many of the Jinn families still harbored resentment against the humans who had enslaved them in magic lamps for thousands of years. It had taken Ben fighting side by side with Gene in the war with Curseworks to finally gain the Jinn's friendship and trust.

"Once when I was little, my cousin Little Gene dared my sister and me to tell our real names to some human kids who lived next door. When my dad found out about it, he totally freaked out." Gene grimaced at the memory. "My cousin was never allowed to come over to our house again."

"Wow, your cousin sounds a lot like mine. She's a real pain," Ben said.

Nora glanced at Ben curiously. "I didn't know that you had a cousin." She leaned forward, intrigued. "What's she like?"

Ben wrinkled his nose. "Penelope? Well, for one thing, she's totally spoiled. My uncle and aunt get her whatever she wants, and usually it's something stupid, pink, and fluffy."

Gene chuckled. "How old is she? Six?"

"That's the thing. She's, like, eleven or twelve now, and last I heard she's still into that stuff. She spent an awful summer with us a while back. She threw horrible temper tantrums, like holding her breath until she passed out and smashing stuff around the house. She even trapped our cat when nobody was looking and lit its whiskers on fire."

Ben shook his head and placed a hand under his chin. "My mom couldn't stand her. By the time the summer was over, she vowed to never have her over again and told my aunt that maybe Penelope should see a psychiatrist." Ben shrugged and continued. "They hardly spoke again after that. I guess that's why after my parents died, my uncle and aunt refused to take me in and I had to go stay at Pinch's Home for Wayward Boys."

Jonathan whistled softly through his teeth and looked at Ben sympathetically. "Well, it was probably for the best. Sounds to me like you would've been miserable living there."

Nora nodded and squeezed Ben's arm. "Besides, it all worked out okay. You've got us now."

Ben smiled at his friends. He had to agree. He had never had such great friends—but still, deep in his heart, he knew that something was missing. A day didn't go by that he didn't think about his parents and how much he wanted to see them again.

*WHOOOP! WHOOOP! WHOOOOOOOP!*

A loud, wailing siren suddenly burst from Ben's watch. All the chattering diners were stunned into silence and looked over at Ben's table with startled faces.

"What's going on?" Gene asked.

Ben pressed a button on the side of his watch and the wailing stopped. A tiny map appeared on the watch face with a pulsing red *X* and the word INTRUDER written above it in bold letters.

"It says there's an intruder near the south wall!"

Ben jumped up and rushed from the table, calling back over his shoulder.

"I think somebody's attacking the Factory!"

# Chapter Two

## Attack of the Spider Monkeys

**B**en grabbed his Battlerang from his back pocket as he dashed down the winding cobblestone streets. "This way!" he shouted to Gene, Jonathan, and Nora as he watched the red *X* on his watch move rapidly to the left side of the tiny map of Wishworks.

Using his watch as a guide, Ben cut across the open field next to the Feathered Funicula tower. He turned left and maneuvered the group through the twisting alleyways, passing many of the quaint shops that were spread throughout the sprawling Factory.

Moments later, they found themselves in a deserted area about fifty yards from the Factory's southern wall. To his alarm, Ben saw a small group of monsters dragging a bound and gagged figure behind them.

*Spider Monkeys!* Even though they were far away, Ben recognized the evil soldiers of the Curseworks Army.

"Who have they got?" Ben whispered urgently to Jonathan, who was peering through a collapsible telescope he'd had in his pocket.

"I'm trying to make out the face . . . one second," the tall boy whispered back as he twisted the focus on the scope. After a moment Jonathan shouted with surprise, "It's a Jinn child!"

Hearing Jonathan's startled cry, the Spider Monkeys wheeled around and spotted them.

"Oh, great. Here they come!" Nora said, clutching leprechaun-size Battlerangs in each hand. Immediately, a large group of the creatures scuttled forward, their barbed spears leveled. Ben noticed that the three Spider Monkeys dragging the Jinn were trying to escape down a tunnel entrance near the edge of the wall.

"You guys take the main group! I'll make sure the others don't get away!"

With Jonathan, Gene, and Nora distracting most of the

Spider Monkeys, Ben dashed to the tunnel entrance and lowered himself down. Once inside, Ben noticed pickaxes and shovels scattered on the dirt floor. He carefully made his way around the tools, trying to move quietly. *I'll bet they dug this all the way from Curseworks,* he thought as he crept forward nervously.

Ben scanned the gloom but couldn't see any sign of the prisoner. Suddenly, out of the corner of his eye, Ben saw something move. As he wheeled around, a heavily armored Spider Monkey emerged from a side passage that had been concealed by the shadows. The creature swung a sword at Ben's head, almost knocking off his oversize stovepipe hat.

*"Whoa!"* Without pausing to think, Ben hurled his Battlerang at the monster. With a piercing scream, the Spider Monkey reeled backward and crumpled to the ground.

"That was close," Ben admitted to himself shakily and fitted his hat more firmly on his head. He returned the Battlerang to his back pocket. It still felt warm from the burst of energy that it produced whenever it made contact with an enemy.

Ben took a deep breath and moved on. His eyes scanned the gloom ahead and he strained to hear any sound that might another enemy.

en, a howl split the air. Two Spider Monkeys

emerged from the shaft in front of him, scuttling forward with burning eyes. Ben whipped his hand to his weapon. He hoisted the Battlerang back, preparing to throw. But the weapon flew out of his sweaty hand and disappeared somewhere in the darkness behind him.

*No!* Ben stumbled backward as the two Spider Monkeys advanced with their curved swords drawn. Ben reached to his back pocket for his spare Battlerang, then suddenly remembered that he had left it back at his cottage earlier that morning.

"Uh-oh." Ben grabbed the edge of his watch and randomly pressed some of the many buttons, hoping that one of them would activate the two-way radio feature. He desperately wished he had taken the time to study the instruction booklet. He held down one of the larger brass knobs and shouted into the watch face.

"Thom, it's Ben! Are you there?"

There was no response from the other end.

The hulking Spider Monkeys sliced their swords in sweeping arcs toward Ben, forcing him backward down the tunnel.

*Swish!* Ben barely ducked each sweeping blow. The Spider Monkeys were not great swordsmen, but they were definitely getting too close for comfort. Without his Battlerang, Ben didn't stand a chance!

Suddenly a blinding flash of light filled the tunnel.

It took Ben a moment to make out the silhouette of a tall figure wearing a derby and holding a pocket watch. The monkeys stopped their advance, stunned by the arrival of the unexpected newcomer.

"Catch!"

Ben smoothly grabbed the Battlerang that Thomas Candlewick tossed to him. Not wasting a second, Ben hurled the weapon, ricocheting the Battlerang off of the first creature's battered helmet in a shower of sparks and sending the spinning weapon hurtling into the second one in an incredible bank shot. The two Spider Monkeys screeched as the weapon sliced through their rusted armor. Ben snatched the returning Battlerang out of the air and returned it to his back pocket. "I guess you heard me," Ben said to Candlewick. He was grateful that his desperate cries into his watch had brought some help.

Candlewick smiled grimly. "Your watch sent out a distress signal when you radioed for help. Mine automatically picked it up and I transported myself here." He glanced down at the fallen Spider Monkeys. "Looks like I was just in time." He glanced over at Ben's wrist. "Yours has the same feature, you know. You could have transported yourself somewhere else."

Ben looked amazed. "It all happened too fast. Besides," he said sheepishly, "I don't know how. I haven't gotten that far in the manual yet[7]."

Candlewick laid a firm hand on Ben's shoulder. "Next time let me know before you jump into a situation like this. I don't want you to get hurt."

Ben nodded.

"And by the way . . ." Candlewick reached down and picked up the Battlerang Ben had let slip out of his hand earlier. "Always carry a spare, okay?"

Ben blushed, knowing that Candlewick was right. He should have prepared more carefully that morning.

Candlewick scowled as he glanced down at the fallen Spider Monkeys. "I can't believe Thornblood would pull a stunt like this."

If there was one thing Ben knew, it was that the president of Curseworks couldn't be trusted. Even though Wishworks had defeated Curseworks in the war six months ago, Adolfus Thornblood was never known to play by the rules.

---

[7] In fairness to Ben, the owner's manual that accompanies an O'Doyle Magical Timepiece resembles an entire set of encyclopedias. Very few people have actually read the entire thing, preferring instead to stumble upon many of the watch's special features through trial and error. This method has resulted in several accidental magical mishaps, including turning one president temporarily into a butternut squash.

"That's not all," Ben said quietly as he moved farther down the narrow passageway. "Look."

In the shadowy tunnel, the Jinn child that had been kidnapped by the Spider Monkeys was huddled up in a protective ball. Ben judged that she couldn't have been more than five or six years old—and was likely scared out of her wits.

Candlewick rushed to the Jinn's side. Using the heated blade from Ben's Battlerang, he cut away her bonds. When the Jinn was free, Candlewick looked deeply into her eyes and spoke soothingly in a language Ben couldn't understand. He assumed that it was Jinnish[8], the Jinns' native tongue.

The girl seemed to appreciate whatever it was Candlewick said to her. Ben could tell that she was beginning to relax, because the color of the smoke trail that extended from her torso turned from an agitated crimson to a soothing blue.

*Da-da dum dum, daa doo* . . . The lilting, electronic strains of the "Happy Birthday" song interrupted their conversation. Candlewick removed a gold-plated cell phone from his jacket and answered.

---

[8] The Jinnish language is divided into two types, Everyday Jinnish and High Jinni. The language is exceptionally complicated: Some words have up to fifty meanings depending on how they're used. As a result, conversational Jinnish was adopted so that humans could communicate with Jinns on a basic level. Refer to the guide at the end of this book for some simple phrases.

"This is Thom." He gestured for Ben to take the Jinn girl out of the tunnel.

Ben smiled at the child and offered his hand.

"Hi, I'm Ben."

"Jeannie," the girl said, shaking his hand.

Ben helped the young Jinn hover through the passageway and emerge into the bright daylight outside.

Once out of the tunnel, Ben was relieved to see that his friends had been triumphant in their battle, too.

"Are you guys okay?" Ben asked, approaching the group with the little Jinn in tow.

"Fine," Nora answered. "But Jonathan's gonna have a shiner tomorrow." She pointed at a nasty red spot near his eye.

Jonathan shrugged. "It could have been worse, believe me. Is she okay?" Jonathan crouched down and smiled kindly at the Jinn girl.

"She's a little shaken up, but seems all right," Ben replied. "Thom talked to her a bit and I think that calmed her down." The girl offered Jonathan a shy smile while still holding tightly to Ben's hand. Gene began to converse with her in Jinnish. After a moment he translated for the rest of the group.

"She says that her mother sent her to the store on an errand when the Spider Monkeys grabbed her. She was really scared and wanted to say thank you to Ben for coming to rescue her."

The girl raised both of her tiny hands toward Ben in a prayerlike gesture, bowing her head slightly and saying, "*M'nud, m'hari.*"

"In our language it means, 'I'm thankful for the Spirit that makes you breathe,'" Gene said, smiling.

Ben smiled at the girl and tried to imitate the gesture, the words coming awkwardly to his tongue. The little Jinn seemed to understand and beamed up at him.

"Not bad," Gene said with a wink. "Maybe I'll have to start teaching you Jinnish."

Moments later, a very serious-looking Candlewick emerged from the tunnel and greeted the small group. After checking to make sure that everyone was okay, he turned to Ben and said, "That was Perkins on the phone. He says that Rottenjaw, the Curseworks attorney, is on his way over to discuss the incident."

He laid a hand on Ben's shoulder. "I want you to come with me to the meeting. Thornblood's attack violates the truce he signed six months ago. Not only that, but to kidnap a Jinn is unthinkable!" Candlewick's expression hardened. "His attorney has a lot of explaining to do."

# ≋ CHAPTER THREE ≋

## Rottenjaw

"What Mr. Thornblood wants is advantageous for both parties, I assure you. All we're looking for is a bit of magical help to speed the process along." The balding attorney, wearing a long black cloak and an expensive-looking vest, peered over his small oval spectacles as he spoke. "The loan of one of the Jinn servants from your factory would have hardly made a difference to you. After all, you do have thousands of Jinns working here. I assure you, my client didn't think that you would object."

Ben had been cautioned by Candlewick not to speak up

in the meeting, but he was having difficulty keeping quiet. He couldn't believe the nerve of the request! If his friend Gene had heard Rottenjaw talk about Jinns as if they were servants, he would have punched the guy right in the nose!

It had taken thousands of years to work through the Jinns' distrust of humans for imprisoning them in lamps and forcing them to be their personal slaves.

Ben sank lower into his seat and glared across the long mahogany table at Rottenjaw. Candlewick was seated in the beautifully carved presidential chair that his father, Leo Snifflewiffle, had once occupied.

Shortly after his retirement as president, Leo had passed away. Ben knew that the passing had been hard on Candlewick, but he had noticed it had also changed him. Where he used to be a workaholic, these days Candlewick took more and more time out of his busy work schedule to spend with Ben. Ben didn't complain. He really looked up to Candlewick and was grateful for the time that they spent together.

"Mr. Rottenjaw, every Jinn employed by our factory is an individual with his or her own mind," Candlewick argued coolly. "They're not slaves that are required to do our bidding. They're all here by their own free will."

Rottenjaw responded silkily, bowing his head in apology.

"Of course, I didn't mean to imply . . ."

Candlewick's voice rose, interrupting. "I know your boss. Although he hates to admit it, he was a former intern of mine[9] and I've watched him in action. There is no doubt in my mind that he'd try to use the Jinn's magic to launch another attack on Wishworks. Hear me now, Mr. Rottenjaw." Candlewick leaned toward the attorney and gave him a pointed look. "Adolfus Thornblood has been dying to get his hands on Jinn magic for years. We both know he can dismantle his curse-making machinery the same way he put it together, by using those foul Spider Monkeys of his. He won't get any help from Wishworks. And if he ever attempts to kidnap another Jinn"—Candlewick's eyes glittered—"I will take that as a declaration of war."

*"Kidnap?"* Rottenjaw sounded offended. "Mr. Candlewick, you cannot possibly prove—"

"I have a witness right here." Candlewick indicated Ben with a nod. "And I trust my department manager's word on the matter. Is that understood?"

---

[9] Many people have wondered at Candlewick's choice of Adolfus Thornblood as a Factory intern fifteen years ago. When asked about it later, Candlewick's standard reply has been, "He had a decent résumé and referral letters. How was I to know that he was secretly a demented monster?" Insiders have speculated, however, that Candlewick might have actually known what Thornblood was capable of and wanted to reform him. Obviously, it didn't work.

Rottenjaw contemplated the implied threat. "I'll inform my client of your decision," the attorney stated, breaking the silence.

Ben glared up at the man with tight-lipped dislike. He had held his tongue until now, but he couldn't hold it one second longer. He blurted out, "Does Thornblood pay you to be such an arrogant jerk, or is that something you do for free?"

Rottenjaw shot Ben a cold, appraising look.

Ben silently dared him to respond. After a moment, the attorney sneered and swept from the room with his black silk cloak billowing behind him.

Candlewick closed the conference room door and Ben growled, "That guy is such a liar."

Candlewick nodded absently. "Yeah, I know. But still, you have to remember to control yourself. A guy like that is just waiting for you to let your emotions get the best of you. He'll use every word you say against you. It's why Thornblood hired him. He's a shark, Ben. You've got good instincts about people, and that's important in a leader, but you've got to stay calm. A very intelligent man once said, 'Be wise as a serpent and gentle as a dove.' It would be a good idea to remember that."

Ben nodded sheepishly. He knew Candlewick was right

and regretted his outburst. The last thing that he wanted to do was to make Candlewick think he wasn't up to the job. He vowed to be more careful in the future.

Candlewick gave Ben's shoulder a friendly squeeze. "We'll hit Battlerang practice later and you can get all your aggression out there. Just remember to play it cool from now on and you'll be fine. "

He produced his pocket watch, glanced at it, and clipped it shut in a businesslike manner. "We'd better get going. There's a little girl who just made a birthday wish for a lot of money. And you are going to make her wish come true."

# ≋ CHAPTER FOUR ≋

## *The Cornucopia*

**M**achinery whirred and hummed as Ben and Candlewick walked down the pathway that led through the Fulfillment department. Ben loved this part of the Factory and visited frequently on his lunch breaks, fascinated by the process of wish formation and fulfillment.

Workers wearing bright Wishworks coveralls managed the control knobs, focusing the blurry images that had recently arrived from the Thaumaturgic Cardioscope. Several large screens depicting various scenes of girls and boys blowing out candles flickered above the technicians' heads. The workers tried to determine whether or not all of the wishing rules had been followed. If the wisher did it right, then a small Wishing Card was directed over to Ben's office. His job was to then make sure that the wish was fulfilled.

"Hi, Delores." Candlewick walked up to a pretty brunette working at one of the stations.

"Oh, Thom, you startled me." She blushed.

"Oops, sorry. I thought you heard me coming."

Ben noticed that the normally confident Candlewick seemed uncomfortable and kept fiddling with his pocket-watch chain.

"Um, so . . . how's the processing going?"

Delores smiled, her full lips curling upward prettily. "Very well. I just finished processing the wish you asked for and sent it up to the Cornucopia with Perkins."

"Oh, great. That's good."

Ben stared at them, feeling amused. It was obvious that they liked each other. Candlewick studied a large green tube that stretched up to the ceiling just over Delores's shoulder, too shy to make eye contact. After a few moments of this, he cleared his throat and said, "You know, you really did an amazing job last month. I checked the status report and you were the top processor for the third time in a row."

Delores grinned and patted Candlewick's arm playfully.

"Well, you know me. I love doing what I do."

Candlewick gazed into Delores's eyes for a long moment. Finally, looking a bit dazed, he broke the silence, clearing his throat. "Well . . . we'll, uh, just go on up, then." He motioned for Ben to follow. "See you later, Delores."

"Bye." Delores gave Candlewick a small wave and turned her bright smile in Ben's direction. "Good morning, Mr. Piff." She gave him a wink. Now it was Ben's turn to feel his cheeks warm under the pretty woman's gaze.

"Morning." Ben gave her a quick wave and trotted after Candlewick.

"What was that all about?" Ben jibed, elbowing him in the ribs.

"What? Oh, you mean back there with Delores?" Candlewick's eyes glazed over as he looked back at the corridor of twisting pipes that led to Delores's station. "Nothing, I was just . . . checking in, that's all."

Ben gave Candlewick a knowing grin. "Okay, sure. Whatever you say." Candlewick cleared his throat again and turned his attention to the large brass door before them.

"How come I never knew about this place before?" Ben asked. The door looked like it had been taken from a submarine. Brass rivets decorated the perimeter, and a porthole made of dark green glass was positioned at about eye level.

"Because it wasn't time yet." Candlewick removed a big, old-fashioned key from his key ring. "This is yours. Only three people have a key to this door: you, my assistant Perkins, and me. The lock on this door is practically invincible, immune to most types of magic. You're going to need access to this room if you're going solo from now on."

"Cool!" Ben's heart leaped with excitement. He couldn't wait to get started on his first mission. He had spent months studying up on the many unusual demands wishers had put upon birthday wish managers over the centuries. Ben remembered one in particular, when Department Manager Cecil Flappfoot had tried to deliver a five-hundred-pound butterfly to a little girl with disastrous results.[10] After Ben had read about him, he realized that being manager of Kids' Birthday Wishes Ages 3 to 12 could be a much more dangerous job than it sounded.

---

[10] "Don't pull a Flappfoot" became a popular term at Wishworks whenever a coworker did something that his or her peers thought shortsighted or stupid. Cecil Flappfoot, a newly appointed wish manager, insisted on delivering the gigantic butterfly to a remote address in New York City, completely oblivious to the fact that he was wearing a floral-print Hawaiian shirt at the time. The insect, when released from its immense crate, was hungry and, seeing no other flowers about, took one look at Cecil's shirt and attacked him immediately. Flappfoot later filed for disability insurance at the Factory, claiming that the giant bug's attempt to suck out "nectar" through his nose had left him permanently scarred both physically and emotionally.

Candlewick indicated that Ben should put the key in the lock. The big lock was hard to turn, but Ben persisted and finally, with a loud *clunk*, the chambers fell into place.

Ben was totally unprepared for the sight that met his eyes.

The room they entered had a cathedral ceiling that stretched up higher than an airplane hangar. The dark wooden walls were hung with colorful shields, each one bearing an intricate symbol. Many of the symbols looked like party favors. Ben stood awestruck beneath a large blue shield depicting three green party balloons when he heard Candlewick's voice echo over in his direction.

"Those are the heraldic crests of the past managers. You'll get to pick your own symbol for your crest. Plus, you'll get some business cards with your symbol printed on them after you successfully deliver your first wish. It's an old tradition . . . goes way back[11]."

---

[11] Sir Geoffrey Goodie, birthday wish manager during President Waffletoffee's reign (1235-1310), founded the Secret Order of the Favor, a group that felt sorry for the children who attended a birthday party and had to watch enviously while the lucky person opened their presents. Sir Goodie decided that the other children should have something to look forward to as well. So, the bag of toys and candy generally referred to as a goodie bag, named after the noble knight, was created. The bag of toys is given out at children's birthday parties everywhere to this day. Most wish department managers attend a ceremony to join the Order soon after delivering their first solo wish, and pick a design for their shield in memory of the generous knight.

Ben's mind raced with ideas for a possible crest of his own. "Can we pick whatever we want?" he asked excitedly.

Candlewick nodded. "As long as it has something to do with birthday parties."

Ben noticed that the banner that he had been studying had a plaque with Candlewick's name underneath it. The scrawling type read:

THOMAS CANDLEWICK, MANAGER, KIDS' BIRTHDAY WISHES AGES 3 TO 12, 1999-2007.

Ben wheeled around to call over to Candlewick. "Hey, this one's yours . . ."

But the words died in his throat. He couldn't believe that he hadn't noticed the submarine suspended above him on a huge stone column.

"We're wasting time!" Candlewick called from the sub's deck. He pointed at his pocket watch. "Come on, we've got work to do."

Ben gulped. "Where are we going?"

Candlewick motioned impatiently. "Just come on up. I'll show you when you get here."

Ben wondered how Candlewick had gotten up there so quickly. Making his way past the sparkling water fountains at the base of the giant sub, Ben strode to the long rope ladder that hung down from the ship's deck and stared upward.

*Man, that's high.* Ben felt a twinge of nerves at the prospect of ascending such an unwieldy ladder. *Don't look down.* Placing one foot at a time on the polished mahogany rungs, he climbed slowly upward.

When he reached the top, Candlewick extended a hand and hoisted him up onto the deck. Ben gazed around the ship. It was so cool! The weathered brass surface of the sub glinted dully as beams of colored light fell down from the stained-glass skylight above.

"Amazing," was all Ben could say.

Candlewick chuckled. "Welcome to the Cornucopia. While I was the birthday wish manager, I used to spend every minute I could over here. It was like my second home." He ran a hand over the sub's hull. "She dates back to the time of President Penelope Thicklepick and was one of the inventions that helped to win the First Wishworks War."

Ben gazed at the sub appreciatively. "Does she still run?"

"No. Her engines were damaged during the war, so she was set up here and has been used as an office. I had Delores send the wish you're going to be fulfilling over here this morning."

He motioned for Ben to follow and they moved over to a short ladder that led to the submarine hatch. After Candlewick turned the wheel to unlock the portal, they climbed inside and Ben got his first glimpse of the interior of the amazing sub.

Burgundy curtains with long, golden tassels decorated the walls, reminding Ben of pictures he'd seen once of a nineteenth century English study. As they walked along the interior of the sub, Ben admired the fish tanks filled with interesting sea creatures glowing from tiny alcoves set throughout the cabinetry.

Candlewick led the way past the lavish furnishings to a room in the ship's transom labeled "Captain's Quarters." A familiar voice called, "I've got it all loaded up and ready to go."

The voice belonged to Perkins, Candlewick's portly old friend and assistant, but Ben was puzzled when he heard a second voice, this one with a lilting Irish accent, chime in. "It's about time you got here. What took you so long, anyway?"

# ≋ CHAPTER FIVE ≋

## Sasha's Birthday Wish

"**W**hat are you doing here?" Ben stared at the leprechaun sitting at a large round table with surprise.

Nora grinned and raised an eyebrow at Perkins, who said, "He doesn't know yet." Perkins adjusted his bifocals and looked over the top of them at Ben with a twinkle in his eye. "Meet your new assistant."

"Don't you be getting any ideas about bossing me around or anything. I'm only here because they forced me to do it." Nora smirked, shaking her tiny finger up at Ben.

"Don't you believe it," Candlewick said. "As soon as she

found out about your promotion to birthday wish manager, she sent me e-mails threatening to quit if I didn't give her the job."

Now Ben understood why Nora had acted so mysteriously at the Pot o' Gold earlier that day when he'd talked about going on his first solo mission. He moved to the other side of the table where the leprechaun sat and plopped down in the chair next to hers. "Maybe you can keep me from getting into too much trouble around here."

She grinned and gave Ben a friendly punch on the arm.

Perkins inserted a Wishing Card into an elaborate brass console. Moments later, a small viewing screen raised into view.

"Let's roll it," Candlewick said.

The lights in the captain's quarters dimmed. An image of a little girl poised over her cake, about to make her birthday wish, flickered into view.

"Her name is Sasha Le Chance, and this is her eleventh birthday. Watch closely now."

Ben watched as the girl kept her eyes tightly shut, concentrating on the wish. Candlewick's voice was filled with admiration. "When Delores showed me this one earlier, I was really impressed with how well she followed the wishing rules. For starters, just look at how clearly she visualizes the wish in her head! It's a perfect example of rule number one."

A thought balloon, only visible through the sensitive Thaumaturgic Cardioscope's imaging device, showing a briefcase filled with hundred-dollar bills appeared above her head.

"One million dollars. Every bill imagined just as crisp and clear as can be." Candlewick folded his arms and smiled, shaking his head. Ben was impressed. Most kids didn't follow the wishing rules with such precision. He had seen plenty of kids blow it by not visualizing what they were wishing for firmly enough.

"Okay, watch now. Here come the candles."

Ben found himself subconsciously cheering the girl on, wanting to see how well she executed rule number two: blowing out all the candles with one breath.

Sasha gazed at the candles for a moment, seemingly enjoying the way the flames danced above the cake, before taking a very deep breath.

*Whooooosh!* In one magnificent breath, without a single cough or sputter, she extinguished the blaze completely.

"Wow!" Ben and the others couldn't help clapping their hands. This girl was *good.*

"Okay, now for the tough part. Let's see how she does."

Ben watched as the typical post-wish drama unfolded around the birthday girl. Rule number three clearly stated that if she told anyone what she wished for, everything would be ruined.

Immediately, her well-meaning parents began their interrogation, but Sasha kept her lips tightly pursed together and shook her head forcefully, refusing to say a word.

"Just look at that determination." Candlewick smiled and glanced at Ben. "Reminds me of someone."

Ben grinned. When he had made his wish for unlimited wishes on his last birthday, he had done the same thing.

Ben was still amazed at how many kids instinctively followed the rules and got their birthday wishes to come true. The rules were kept top secret, and no Factory employee was allowed to coach or communicate the rules to any child. If word on the street got out that there was a formula for making wishes come true, even the power of a thousand Jinns wouldn't be able to fulfill them all.

The film flickered to a stop and the lights came back on. "Well, Perkins, this is it." Candlewick looked over at Perkins, who had his arms crossed and was smiling broadly. "Do you think he can handle it?"

Ben was so excited he could hardly stand it. "I'm ready. What do I have to do? Is Nora going with me?" The words tumbled from his lips in a rush.

Candlewick chuckled. "Nora is going to drive the sweepstakes company limo that carries you to deliver the check for one million dollars."

Ben looked concerned. "Yeah, but who's going to believe that a kid is some kind of sweepstakes official? Shouldn't a grown-up do the job?"

Perkins spoke up. "Ah, that's what the Disguise and Prop department is for." His eyes twinkled merrily as he rose from the table. "If you'll follow me, I think I know just the disguise for your trip."

# ≈ CHAPTER SIX ≈
### The Disguise and Prop Department

"**W**hoa." Ben patted his large walrus mustache with his new massive hand. Gazing into the reflection cast by the tall mirror, he watched, astounded, as the face of a balding, fortyish man copied his every move.

"This is our typical sweepstakes delivery guy," Perkins said. "Thom used him a couple of times as an airline pilot, too."

Ben slowly slid the suit jacket from his shoulders and grinned as the image in front of him shimmered back into his regular reflection. "Man, what an amazing coat!" Ben held the ordinary-looking jacket in front of him and gazed at the endless rack of coats.

"We've got just about every disguise you could think of in here. Clowns, waitresses, construction workers, hot dog vendors, you name it." Candlewick indicated the immense walls that were covered with fake beards, mustaches, clown noses, glasses, and hats of every possible size and type. Ben noticed one costume that looked like a dog catcher's uniform.

"A dog catcher? What's that for?"

Perkins answered. "We get wishes every day from people around the world who want their lost pets to come back home. The dog catcher disguise works great for showing up at their houses with missing pets." Perkins adjusted his glasses.

"Do leprechauns and Jinns use this stuff, too?" Ben asked.

"They don't really need these props and costumes. They can use magic to assume whatever form they need to," Candlewick explained. "However, the Jinns created coats like you're wearing to use when ordinary makeup won't do the trick."

Candlewick stroked his long chin and his expression turned serious. "Just remember, whatever you do, don't take off that coat while you're making your delivery. It's absolutely imperative that you're not spotted by anybody." He looked apprehensive. "Keeping the wish fulfillment a secret is an essential part of making the magic work here at the Factory. Promise me that you will be careful."

Ben nodded. "Okay."

Candlewick counted off a checklist on his fingers. "Okay, so, let's go over your secret identity. Your name is Charlie Pantsworth and you work for the Susquehanna Sweepstakes Company."

"Check."

"You are pleased to present this check for one million dollars to whom?"

"Sasha Le Chance."

"Good. Now, let's take a look at your new watch." Candlewick was acting like a nervous parent teaching his son to drive a car.

"What's this button for?" Ben pointed to a small red button on the side of his watch.

Candlewick replied, "That's the button you press to enter into Earth's reality." He scratched his nose. "It's kind of complicated, scientifically speaking. But it will allow you to enter that dimension from any door you choose. I usually try to pick an entryway that nobody would suspect, like an old garage, toilet, chimney, or a beat-up door to a toolshed. You get the idea."

Candlewick nodded over to Nora, who had tried on

one of the coats and was now laughing hysterically at her reflection in the mirror: a tall, pudgy Hawaiian tourist with a loud floral shirt, black socks, and a big black camera hanging on a strap around his neck. She took off the jacket and shimmered back to her normal size.

"Nora will be disguised as a limo driver, and you both will materialize out of an old garage I know about on the east side of Portland."

"Sounds good," Ben said. Then, leaning in confidentially to Candlewick, he asked, "She does know how to drive a car, doesn't she?"

Perkins answered. "We've got that covered. The limo drives itself." Behind them, Nora had put on another jacket, one that made her look like a ballerina with pixie wings and a beard, and was cracking herself up again. Perkins chuckled softly. "I doubt that she has a license."

Candlewick's features were tense and anxious as he put a hand on Ben's shoulder. "I have total faith in you." Ben didn't think Candlewick looked very confident, and for the first time Ben felt nervous himself. A lot was riding on this mission.

Candlewick hesitated before continuing. "If there's any emergency, just go back to the limo and I—"

"I will take it from there, Mr. Candlewick," Nora

interrupted, striding up to them. She gave Ben a huge smile. "Don't worry. I've done this before. I won't let him get into trouble."

As Ben followed Nora to the garage where the limo was kept, he glanced down at the tiny birthday-candle hands of his watch, noting the time.

*Here we go,* Ben thought, his stomach fluttering. *This is my big chance.*

# CHAPTER SEVEN

## The Sweepstakes Winner!

**B**en's knuckles were white as he gripped his briefcase handle with both hands. "Okay, Nora, are you ready?"

The leprechaun adjusted her seat belt. She had magically disguised herself as a glamorous-looking limo driver in her mid-thirties. After applying a generous amount of lipstick, she turned to Ben and nodded. "Ready."

Ben pushed the button on his watch. A thunderous crack split the air and white light crackled all around the car. Ben felt his skin prickle with magical energy as the limousine passed smoothly through a tunnel of white light and materialized in an abandoned garage.

With a loud groan, the heavy, chipped garage door rose, letting in a stream of daylight and revealing an empty alleyway outside. It was the first time in six months that Ben had been back on earth, and he was surprised at how gray and dingy everything looked compared to the sparkling city in which he now lived.

"Try not to be nervous." Nora chuckled, noticing Ben's anxious expression in the rearview mirror. "Your disguise is hilarious, by the way."

The limo turned a corner and drove into a residential neighborhood. Finally, it stopped at a tree-lined driveway next to a mailbox with the name LE CHANCE written across it in big bold letters.

*I can do this,* Ben thought, taking a deep breath.

"Now remember, stay calm and everything will be okay. Just stick to the plan and keep in mind the stuff that Thom told you." Nora adjusted her limo driver's hat in the rearview mirror and scowled at her reflection. "Let's get this over with so that I can get back to my old self again. I look as ridiculous as you do."

Nora opened the door for Ben and stood at attention as he exited the limo. As he strode to the porch and wiped his damp palms on his long trouser legs, he repeated Candlewick's instructions over and over in his mind.

*My name is Charlie Pantsworth. The girl's name is Sasha. I'm with the Susquehanna Sweepstakes Company. My name is Charlie Pantsworth. The girl's name is Sasha. My name is Charlie Pantsworth, the girl's name is Sasha. Hi, I'm Charlie Pantsworth, is your daughter Sasha at home? Charlie Pantsworth. Sasha. Charlie Pantsworth. Sasha. My name is Charlie Pantsworth, I have something for your daughter, Sasha.*

The front door swung open abruptly to reveal a scowling, harried-looking woman with tousled red hair. "Can I help you?"

Ben's mind went blank.

"My name is Party Chanceworth. I have something for your daughter, Shelly."

He was sweating much more than he thought possible! The woman stared at him, confused and skeptical.

After an awkward pause, Ben remembered the briefcase he carried that held the check. He fumbled with the locks for a moment, then produced the envelope. Mrs. Le Chance studied it quizzically for a moment, then said flatly, "There must be a mistake. I didn't enter any . . ."

"Congratulations. She's w-won!" Ben forced a big smile as he handed her the prizewinning envelope.

"Who is it, Mom?" Eleven-year-old Sasha Le Chance bounced into the entryway, looking expectant. "What did I win?" With a quick swipe she grabbed the envelope from her mother's fingers and opened it.

"MOM, LOOK!"

Sasha stared excitedly at the check for a million dollars.

"Let me see that." Mrs. Le Chance took the check and examined it closely, then glanced sharply up at the sweaty, uncomfortable-looking man that stood in front of her. "Is this some kind of joke?"

Ben shook his head quickly and was about to reply when Mr. Le Chance appeared from inside the house, several cameras hanging around his neck. "What's going on?"

Sasha waved the check excitedly. "Dad! I won a million dollars!"

"What?" Mr. Le Chance grabbed the check and read it, then looked pointedly at Ben.

"Is this for real, mister?"

Ben nodded.

"Woo-hoo!" Mr. Le Chance shouted and gestured to his daughter. "Sash, go stand over there by the guy at the door. Let's get a shot of both of you together."

*Uh-oh,* Ben thought as he remembered Candlewick's admonition to avoid leaving any trace of his visit. Even

though he was in disguise, he still didn't want to risk being photographed.

"That's okay, I've gotta get back to the office . . ." Ben said in a deep, gruff voice as he waved his hand in protest.

Mr. Le Chance ignored him and snapped several photos.

"Please, don't. I don't like having my picture taken."

Ben lowered his head behind his hand, shielding his face from the camera. But Mrs. Le Chance was now convinced that something was fishy and pelted Ben with questions.

"We didn't enter any sweepstakes. Who are you? What was the name of the company you said you work for?" she demanded.

Ben pulled his magic coat up over his head, trying desperately to keep Mr. Le Chance from getting a clear shot of his face.

"Hey, come on, mister, just one picture. The guys down at the *News Chronicle* will never believe this!" Mr. Le Chance circled Ben, trying to get a peek beneath his coat. Mrs. Le Chance advanced on Ben's right side, still demanding answers to her questions.

"You didn't answer me. What is the name of the company you said you worked for?"

Ben panicked. This was not going according to the plan! He struggled to remember the name of the company

Candlewick had given him. *What was it?* Unable to control his rising panic, he blurted the first name that popped into his mind.

"The, uh, Wish Factory Sweepstakes . . ."

Turning quickly to avoid the probing camera, he tripped on the white picket fence that surrounded some bushes by the front door. As he fell, he was aware of his coat snagging on the fence.

*R-I-I-I-P!*

Ben's stomach sank as he heard the cloth give way, and the magic jacket was torn from his body.

Mr. and Mrs. Le Chance stared dumbfounded at the small figure that suddenly shimmered into view in front of them.

Flashes from Mr. Le Chance's camera followed Ben as he raced back to the waiting limo.

Nora glanced up from the *Zoom's Academy* comic book she was reading in time to see Ben, his face flushed, carrying the tattered coat and motioning desperately for her to start the engine.

With a squeal of rubber, the limo sped from the driveway and down the street, leaving a bewildered Le Chance family in its wake.

It was only after they had turned a corner at the edge

of town that Ben released his grip on the door handle and slumped back into his seat. Why had he panicked? This was his big chance and he'd totally blown it. Feeling suddenly sick to his stomach, he stared down at the tattered magic jacket that was lying in a heap on the floor of the limo.

Nora, still in her limo driver's disguise, looked back at him sympathetically. She hesitated, and then said, "I'm sure everything will work out okay . . . Thom will understand. I think . . ."

Her voice trailed off as she tried to give Ben a reassuring smile.

Ben stared out the window at the passing cars, feeling miserable. As the Wishworks limousine retraced the streets it had traveled back to the abandoned garage, the gloomy Portland sky darkened and the first few drops of a rainstorm hit the windshield.

Ben listened to the *thump, thump, thump* of the moving wipers as they slid gently back and forth against the window. He absently studied a single drop that fell and then quickly vanished under the rhythmic movement of the wipers.

Only one single, unhappy thought echoed over and over in his head.

*What will Thom say when I get back up to Wishworks?*

# ≋ CHAPTER EIGHT ≋

## Penelope Pauline Piff

"**G**ood evening, and welcome to the Channel Five News at Seven. My name is Libby Sanchez." The pretty anchorwoman shuffled some papers on her news desk and then looked into the camera.

"A mysterious event occurred at the home of an eleven-year-old girl today. Sasha Le Chance, a resident of Portland, Oregon, was shocked at the arrival of a young man bearing a check for one million dollars made out to her."

A slightly blurry picture of Ben flashed on the screen.

"We go now to an exclusive interview with Sadie Le

Chance, the girl's mother."

The camera cut to a prerecorded video of a confused-looking Mrs. Le Chance speaking into a Channel Five News microphone.

"My husband and I went to the bank and found out that the check was genuine, but also discovered that the 'Wish Factory Sweepstakes' doesn't exist. We got Sasha's money—it was funded by an anonymous account somewhere, but I still don't understand it."

Mrs. Le Chance scowled.

"My Sasha didn't enter any sweepstakes that we know of." The woman's tone turned conspiratorial. "And if you want to know the truth, I think the kid might have been some sort of alien from another planet. He could change shape! When he arrived at our door, he looked a lot like my cousin Frank . . ."

The camera turned once more to Libby Sanchez. "Authorities are investigating the strange occurrence, and we will give you live updates as they happen. In other news . . ."

The image of Libby Sanchez suddenly started moving backward. The video news footage rewound until the graphic with Ben's photo filled the screen, frozen in place.

Penelope Pauline Piff pressed the pause button on her remote. Getting up from her pink satin beanbag, clutching a fluffy pink dragon, she shuffled in her pink cashmere slippers to the television and peered closely at the photo. Her blue eyes widened and her long blond braids moved from side to side as she shook her head in disbelief. "It can't be," she breathed.

Penelope put down the remote and slid her closet doors open. She reached into the back of the closet and pulled out a pink-fur-covered photo album.

Then she sat down on her pink satin bed with its pink satin pillows. She put Sweetums, her favorite stuffed dragon, next to her, and began to flip through the photo album.

"Here it is," Penelope said to Sweetums.

She pointed to a photo of herself when she was about seven years old. Seated next to her was none other than a six-year-old Benjamin Piff. A homemade chocolate birthday cake was lit with seven candles and Mr. and Mrs. Piff stood behind their happy son, smiling broadly at the camera.

Penelope had never liked her cousin Ben. That summer five years ago, when she had been forced by her parents to stay with her aunt and uncle, she had done everything she could to try to get them to send her home early, but it hadn't worked.

Travis and Sue (as she called her own parents) were never home, and when they were, Penelope hardly spoke to them at all. It was obvious that her parents lived for one thing only, and that was making money.

Every time they hired a new nanny (which was pretty often, for reasons Penelope couldn't quite understand), the nanny would inevitably comment on the beautiful presents, telling Penelope that she should be thankful to have parents who loved her so much.

Unfortunately, and this was something only Penelope herself knew, there was only one present she wanted from her parents: their time. When she was little, she used to beg them to play with her, but her parents were always too busy to notice.

When she was a bit older, she tried throwing terrible tantrums, imagining that if they scolded her, she'd at least be getting some attention from them. This only made them more distant.

Now, on the eve of her twelfth birthday, she had finally given up on ever spending any time with them. She had resorted to leaving a list of her demands on their respective fax machines at work, insisting on the latest and trendiest outfits, toys, or electronic gadgets that she had seen on TV. Her parents were fine with this arrangement, and they would fulfill Penelope's birthday requests mainly because it would keep Penelope quiet and out of their way.

The arrangement Penelope had with her parents was very different from the way her cousin's family worked. Ben's parents enjoyed spending time with him. The whole family had had a close, loving bond. Knowing this about them had caused her heart to grow as small and hard as one of her diamond-studded hair clips, and it made her angry to see Ben enjoying something that she could never buy, even if she had a billion dollars.

After the airplane crash that took Ben's parents' lives, Ben had been left with no living relatives other than Penelope's family. Ben's parents had been deep in debt, and he had been left without any inheritance at all and no place to live.

A few days later Penelope heard her parents refuse the social worker's pleas to have Ben live with her family, claiming that they were already overwhelmed with one child.

And now that she had seen the frightened face of her cousin on TV, apparently involved in some kind of suspicious activity, she couldn't wait to find out more about what trouble he was up to.

Moving to her computer, she pulled up a search engine and typed in the words *Benjamin Bartholomew Piff*.

Instantly, a result listing Pinch's Home for Wayward Boys showed up.

Penelope clicked the link and read:

*Benjamin B. Piff*
*Resident from 2006-2007*
*Whereabouts: Unknown*

Penelope smiled inwardly. She imagined that her cousin had probably run away from the orphanage and fallen in with some criminals. Maybe even a counterfeiter's ring that ran some kind of mail-order scam that operated under the guise of being a sweepstakes company.

After pondering this for a moment, she typed in the other words she had heard in the news broadcast. The computer took a while to process her request, apparently having a more difficult time finding this information. Finally, a single result showed up:

*Wish Factory*

She clicked the link.

Her computer screen suddenly crisscrossed with a loud plaid design. An electronic bagpipe played a screeching jig as the web page loaded up. Soon, the smiling face of a funny-looking little man in a green suit, smoking a long clay pipe and waving a fist full of dollars in his right hand, filled the screen. The words underneath the picture read:

*"Self-help guru Paddy O'Doyle can help make all of your wishes work for you! For a payment of only one thousand dollars, you,*

*too, can receive his exciting new book that will tell you the secrets to fulfilling all your deepest desires. Mastercard, Visa, and PayPal accepted."*

Penelope wasn't sure if this website was what she was looking for. The site looked kind of cheap, homemade, and more than a little suspicious. She stared at the picture of Paddy O'Doyle for a long moment, trying to figure out what she should do. Then she decided that he looked exactly like the type of guy who would be up to something sneaky and criminal, so she clicked the "Contact Me" button at the top of the page.

*Dear Mr. O'Doyle,*

*My name is Penelope Piff. I am trying to locate my cousin, Benjamin. I have reason to believe that he works for your company, the Wish Factory Sweepstakes.*

*Please help me find him. He is a runaway and needs to be returned to the orphanage to which he belongs.*

*Sincerely,*

*Penelope Piff*

She smiled, imagining the surprise on Ben's face when he was whisked away from wherever he was and put back into Pinch's Home for Wayward Boys. She had barely finished

sending the letter when there was a sudden knock at her front door. Moments later when she opened it, a completely unexpected sight met her eyes. Standing in front of her was the tiny man she had just seen on the website, dressed in an awful-looking maroon and gold suit.

The man glanced at an ornate silver pocket watch and replaced it in his vest pocket. Doffing his tattered green derby, he bowed in front of Penelope and said in a thick Irish accent, "I came as soon as I got your e-mail."

Penelope stared at the strange man, dumbfounded. The little man continued, smiling up at her and revealing a chipped front tooth. "Paddy O'Doyle at your service, Miss Piff."

# ≋ CHAPTER NINE ≋

### Rottenjaw Reports

"**T**hey are unwilling to be persuaded, Mr. Thornblood."

Rottenjaw bowed low before Adolfus Thornblood, who was seated at his rickety, chipped writing desk. Contrary to what had been reported earlier to Candlewick, the president of Curseworks was not on the brink of death, but rather healthy and alert.

Thornblood didn't look up as he replied. "And you told them that I only required the assistance of *one* Jinn to help me dismantle the Factory?"

"Yes, sir."

Thornblood dipped his long quill into the bottle of bloodred ink. "Well, this comes as no surprise, Rottenjaw. Thomas Candlewick may be many things, but he's not ignorant." The tall, skeletal man paused to write a few words on a piece of parchment.

Rottenjaw smoothed the front of his elegant vest and adjusted his small glasses. "With all due respect, Mr. Thornblood, even though we've tried to convince them that you are on the brink of death, they didn't take too kindly to your kidnapping attempt. If we try anything like that again, they might attack us. I suggest that you find another way to get the magical power Curseworks needs."

Thornblood didn't respond for a long time, and Rottenjaw wondered if he had said too much. The face of the president of the once mighty Curseworks Factory twitched as he tried to suppress his barely concealed rage. After mastering himself, he said in a restrained voice, "Mr. Rottenjaw, if I can't get my hands on another Wish Globe capable of producing unlimited wishes, then I must have Jinn magic to power my factory and my curse-making machines. It is your job to discover how that is to be accomplished."

Rottenjaw pretended to inspect his glasses as Thornblood's voice grew dangerously quiet.

"Always remember"—Thornblood raised a bony finger and pointed it at the elegantly dressed attorney—"as long as even one stone of this factory stands, I still have enough power to turn you into one of my spidery servants[12]."

Rottenjaw gritted his teeth and made a little half bow. He hated being threatened by anyone. Through clenched teeth he said softly, "I'll return to Wishworks in the morning."

---

[12] Thornblood's power source that transforms traitorous Wishworks Employees into the twisted, horrible Spider Monkeys has never been discovered, and many rumors abound. Some think that he has a half-starved Jinn imprisoned deep within the Factory that he forces to do his bidding. Others believe that he found a banshee while traveling through the Leprechaun Counties and learned the dark arts of transformation from the evil creature. Still others think he's lying about having any magic at all and is just really good with scissors and tape, creating his own Spider Monkey costumes out of foam, rubber, and glue, and forcing unfortunate employees to wear them. Nobody really knows the truth.

# ≈ CHAPTER TEN ≈
## The Talk

"*I* just don't get it. I thought I explained the whole thing to you very carefully. What happened down there?"

Ben had expected Candlewick to be upset, maybe even angry, but seeing his face so filled with disappointment caught him off guard. It was almost worse than being yelled at.

"I don't know, I just panicked, I guess."

Candlewick rubbed a hand through his graying hair and stared out from the window of his sumptuous office to the lamp-lit streets below.

"Have you seen the news? Do you have any idea how

much trouble this has caused?" Ben had seen the television monitors on almost every employee's desk tuned to Libby Sanchez reporting the news of his bungled delivery.

"I didn't mean to!" Ben said defensively. "That lady down there kept pushing and pushing, and the dad was snapping pictures all over the place. I'm sorry, okay . . . I'm really sorry! You think I meant to say that stuff?"

"I thought you were ready. I guess it was just too soon to make you a department manager." Candlewick sat down at his desk and picked up several pink pieces of paper, all handwritten notes from different departments in the Factory wondering if the rumors about the botched wish delivery were true.

Ben's eyes burned as he stood up and walked over to Candlewick's littered desk. Removing his magic watch from his wrist, he said quietly, "Yeah, well, guess what? If you think you made a mistake in hiring me, then I don't want the job anymore."

Ben's face felt hot as he set his watch down on the edge of Candlewick's desk and marched to the large wooden door that led out of his office.

When he arrived at his tiny cottage a few minutes later, he felt so empty inside that he didn't even take time to stroke Rags, his scruffy puppy. Ignoring the dog's whine for attention, Ben hung his big top hat on the peg near the door and collapsed onto his mattress.

He stared out the window at the Thaumaturgic Cardioscope building. Every night, Ben liked to watch the machine's big gears circle slowly in the lamp-lit darkness, steadily ticking. He had always found the sound comforting, knowing that the machine was always hard at work, listening in on the wishes of people all over the world. It used to make him proud to know that he was lucky enough to work at the Factory, helping to make dreams come true, but now . . .

His eyes burned as he turned over and buried his face in his pillow. *Maybe Thom is right,* Ben thought miserably. *Maybe I'm not cut out to be a wish manager after all.*

# CHAPTER ELEVEN
### Paddy O'Doyle

"*C*an I come in?"

Penelope stood at her front door, unsure of whether or not to let the little man come inside. Her parents were gone on a business trip and had instructed her not to open the door to strangers. Besides, something was fishy. She couldn't understand how he had arrived so quickly after she sent her e-mail. She hadn't even included her address!

Glancing down at him she decided, *He's only as high as my knee, what harm could he do?*

She opened the front door a little wider.

The man grinned and replaced his tattered derby on his head as he stepped inside the marble entryway. Paddy strode into the living room and looked around appreciatively, admiring the fine furniture. He clambered onto the white leather sofa and immediately propped his feet up on the coffee table.

Penelope scowled at the man, certain that her mother would have a fit if she saw him putting his feet on her antique table. "How did you find me, Mr. O'Doyle?"

"Call me Paddy." The man picked at a blackened fingernail as he spoke. "When I got your e-mail, I tuned into you with my magic pocket watch. It can take me anywhere in the world. I knew right away that you needed my help."

Penelope looked dubious. "Magic pocket watch? Are you crazy?"

"No, I'm a leprechaun. I come from a world where wishes come true." He folded his arms defiantly, as if daring her to contradict his statement.

Penelope stared, not knowing whether to laugh or run away. She couldn't deny that he was the smallest person she had ever seen, but she couldn't bring herself to believe that he was really a leprechaun.

Feeling nervous, she said, "Look, let's get something straight. The only thing I wanted was information on my cousin." Penelope crossed her arms, trying to look important. "I want the police to put him back in the orphanage. That's it. I don't want to buy anything." She gave the grizzled little man her best glare.

Paddy chuckled. "You're a girl that probably has had all the things money can buy, but still hasn't a single thing that she could possibly wish for."

He continued before Penelope could respond. "I'll tell you all about your cousin in a minute, but first let me ask you something." He leaned toward her conspiratorially. "What if I told you that there is a factory that could fulfill your deepest wish?" He stared at her intently, his tiny eyes glinting like golden marbles. "Any wish you could imagine, like being able to fly, or to never grow old, or to eat ice cream every day for the rest of your life." He stopped and gave Penelope a crooked smile.

Penelope was suspicious. She had seen door-to-door salesmen try to manipulate her parents before and had a pretty good idea of a sales pitch with a "catch" when she heard one.

"A wish factory?" She scowled and rolled her eyes. "Listen, mister, I don't know where you came from. I admit, you're really small and I don't know how you got here so quickly, but I'm not buying the whole 'magic leprechaun' thing. You probably are just trying to get me to buy some magazine subscriptions or something. Either tell me what I want to know about my cousin, or you're going to have to leave."

She stood up and headed to the front door.

"Wait, wait!" Paddy's smug expression turned desperate. "You need to hear me out. Everything I'm telling you has to do with your cousin." He quickly dashed in front of her and blocked the door.

"Benjamin Piff is the new manager of Kids' Birthday Wishes Ages 3 to 12. He works at the Wishworks Factory."

The grizzled little man looked earnest for the first time since Penelope had started talking to him.

"It's a place powered by wish-fulfilling Jinns that would obey your every command." With that, he reached into his jacket pocket and pulled out a small transparent globe. "This is a Wish Globe. When someone makes a wish, one of these is produced by the Factory. This one is already used; that's why you can't see the wish inside of it."

He handed the globe to Penelope. Raising an eyebrow doubtfully, she examined the glass ball. There was nothing unusual about it. She glanced up at her front door and then down to the little man, wondering if she should try to jump over his head and make a run for it.

As if reading her thoughts, Paddy interrupted.

"And now I'm going to prove it to you."

With a snap of his fingers, the globe that Penelope held flared to life. Dumbfounded, she stared at the castlelike factory that glowed within the tiny bubble.

"How did you . . ." But before she could complete her sentence, the scene changed to reveal a quaint-looking little cottage standing next to a clockwork machine. The scene zoomed in on a window in the cottage, and through the window Penelope could see the tiny figure of her cousin Ben moving about inside.

"It's him," she whispered.

If she had been able to tear her eyes away from the glowing scene in front of her, she would have seen a crafty grin spread across the leprechaun's scruffy face.

"Yes, it's him all right. Your cousin made an incredible wish on his birthday last year, a wish that changed his life forever."

Penelope felt an old and familiar jealousy prick her heart. How could this have possibly happened? Somehow things always seemed to work out for Ben. He always managed to land on his feet.

Here he was—what did the little man say?—"managing" this whole fairy-tale place where wishes came true? It seemed impossible, and yet, she couldn't deny what she was seeing with her own eyes. It seemed too real to be any kind of magic trick.

She tore her eyes from the globe and, turning to the little man, said hesitantly, "Okay. Let's say I believe you. What do we do to make my wish happen?"

"Simple. I'll show you how to do it, and you won't believe how incredibly easy it is. In fact, you'll probably wonder why you never realized how to do it yourself!"

"Okay, let's hear it," Penelope said impatiently.

"Tomorrow's your birthday, right?" Paddy asked.

"How did you know that?" Penelope demanded.

"A trade secret," he replied simply and shrugged. He glanced at his pocket watch. "It's almost midnight. You'll be officially turning twelve in a matter of minutes."

Penelope narrowed her eyes. "Why aren't *you* working at this Wishworks place? You seem to know so much about it."

For the first time, Paddy looked uncomfortable.

"Ah, well, you see, its kind of a long story. I did business there, but I wasn't too happy with the management at the time . . . anyway, that's not the point." The leprechaun's voice softened. "Look, I can't get back up there without your help. All you have to do is follow the rules that I have written down in my book. I only ask for one condition . . ."

He pulled a stapled pamphlet out of his pocket and handed it to Penelope. "When you make your wish to take over the Wishworks Factory, you make me your right-hand man."

Dazed, Penelope gazed down at the tattered pamphlet. She turned the cardstock cover page and read:

## TO MAKE A CHILD'S BIRTHDAY WISH COME TRUE

1.  The child's eyes must be closed while visualizing the wish, and the nature of the wish must be seen clearly in his or her mind.
2.  Every candle must be blown out with one breath. No sputtering, second breaths, or spitting.
3.  Under absolutely no condition, not even under the most intense questioning, should the wish be told to another living soul. This will cancel the wish.

Penelope turned the page, looking for more rules. Seeing that there weren't any more, she lowered the pamphlet and frowned. The whole thing seemed too obvious to be possible. Could it be that the simplest rules in the world could make powerful dreams come true?

She glanced back over at the Wish Globe, noticing that it had returned to its ordinary transparency. If she hadn't seen the amazing factory in the tiny globe, she would have never believed it. It had to be true! Straightening her shoulders, Penelope offered Paddy O'Doyle a determined smile and shook his tiny hand.

"Mr. O'Doyle, you have a deal."

"Excellent!" The little man was so excited, he did a jig on the living room carpet. "Now then." He gazed up at Penelope with a crooked grin. "We need a birthday cake and candles."

The leprechaun strode to the refrigerator and rummaged around inside. Moments later he placed a plate of cold meat loaf on the kitchen table in front of Penelope with a triumphant smile. Penelope stared down at the gooey meat loaf disgustedly.

"Uh, hello? That's not birthday cake," she drawled.

Paddy grinned and snapped his fingers. A sparkle of gold dust settled down on the plate of food. To Penelope's surprise, a wedge of delicious-looking cake with a lit candle on it appeared.

The leprechaun looked up at Penelope with a greedy expression. "Now all you have to do is follow the instructions and make your wish. Remember, nobody can hear exactly what you wished for, or it won't come true."

Penelope glanced at the pamphlet, familiarizing herself with the rules. Closing her eyes, she focused her thoughts and visualized the wish clearly in her mind. *I wish the Wishworks Factory was mine.*

# ᑍ Chapter Twelve ᑌ

## A Rude Awakening

**W**hen Ben woke abruptly the next morning, he had an uneasy feeling in the pit of his stomach. Glancing blearily at the small wind-up alarm clock that sat on the nightstand next to his bed, he noticed that there was still an hour before the time he usually got up. Normally he would have turned over and tried to catch a few more minutes of sleep before work, but he knew instinctively that he wouldn't be able to do that this time if he tried.

He kicked his patchwork quilt to the foot of his bed and walked to his large bedroom window. As he stared at the empty cobblestone street in front of his house, he noticed something was missing . . . something that he couldn't quite put his finger on . . . something obvious . . .

With a start he realized what it was. The gentle ticking sound from the Thaumaturgic Cardioscope had stopped! He couldn't remember a time when it had ever been turned off, not even for a moment. Jonathan said that because the world never stopped wishing, expert technicians were employed around the clock to keep the intricate machine well oiled and trouble free. Something had to be really wrong if the Cardioscope wasn't working!

Ben got dressed quickly and raced across the street to the Thaumaturgic Cardioscope building. He skidded to a stop in front of the place where the entrance doors should have been, but they were gone! How could that be? In place of the doors, there was a solid wall. Panicked, Ben raced around the side of the circular structure, hoping to see a point of entry somewhere. He nearly collided with a figure running in the opposite direction.

"Ben!"

"Jonathan!" Ben cried out, stumbling backward. Jonathan Pickles looked like he hadn't slept all night.

"What's going on?" Ben asked his friend.

"Someone has taken over the Factory and shut down

the Scope." Jonathan's words came out in a rush. "Perkins is forming a secret resistance! I was just coming to get you!"

Icy chills ran down Ben's back.

"I don't understand. Who took over?"

Jonathan glanced up at the big brass ear rising above them. "Nobody knows. But now there are horrible *things* guarding the President's Tower." He shuddered. "They wiped out at least half of the night shift."

Ben's heart beat wildly. Jonathan said, "Perkins wants you, me, Gene, and Nora to meet at the Cornucopia."

Jonathan noted Ben's surprised expression and nodded. "Yeah, I know about it. Perkins said that under the circumstances, the submarine shouldn't be kept a secret. It's in the one place with enough magical protection to withstand whatever danger is thrown at us[13]." Jonathan took hold of Ben's arm. "Let's go."

Ben resisted Jonathan's pull, staring down the winding road to the President's Tower.

"Has anybody seen Thom?"

---

[13] The hangar that holds the Cornucopia was fortified with Jinn spells after the First Wishworks War at great cost to the Factory. The Jinn Union made sure that the workers who supplied the magical protection were paid triple time for their exhaustive efforts, and the resulting debt incurred by the Factory took more than fifty years to repay. This slow payment plan added to the long list of human failures that have contributed to the Jinns' resentment over the years.

Jonathan shook his head. "No, nobody has. Most people think he must be trapped in there with whoever took over."

Ben's face hardened. "Then I'm going to find him."

Jonathan looked horrified. "You can't! Ben, you have no idea how many of those guards are over there."

Ben turned to Jonathan. "He might be in danger!"

Ignoring Jonathan's pleas to reconsider, Ben jerked his arm free and raced back to his cottage. Pocketing his Battlerangs, he ran down the deserted streets toward the Presidential Tower.

He had to find Candlewick. If the Cardioscope had stopped working, then thousands of people weren't being granted their wishes. Candlewick had told him that without the hope that wishes bring, mankind would be doomed.

Ben rushed to the low wall that surrounded the presidential offices. He desperately hoped that it wasn't too late to find his mentor.

# CHAPTER THIRTEEN

## The Horrible Snifters

*B*en peered through the crack in the wall, which gave him a clear view of the Presidential Tower's courtyard. His breath caught in his throat when he observed the monstrous guards that patrolled the door leading to Candlewick's office.

The creatures' pale faces had no features except for long, misshapen noses that sniffed the air expectantly from time to time, as if trying to catch an elusive scent. They had tall fur hats on their heads that reminded Ben of the guards that patrolled outside of Buckingham Palace, and their crooked bodies were draped with richly embroidered green coats that dragged on the flagstones beneath them.

Ben's hand moved shakily to the Battlerang at his belt as he tried to calm his breathing.

He glanced down the side of the wall. To his horror, he saw that a small group of the creatures were bent low to the ground, their long noses sniffing along the trail, tracking him down.

He knew he'd be in trouble if they discovered his hiding spot. Wasting no time, he grabbed the nearest protruding stone on the wall and scrambled upward, hoping to put as much distance between himself and them as possible. Lying flat on top of the wall, he peered over the side and studied the guards, who were now sniffing the spot where he had been standing only moments before.

They circled the spot, probing for a trace of his scent. Then suddenly, to Ben's horror, one of the creatures tilted its fleshy head up at him.

Soundlessly it raised a twisted hand and pointed to Ben, who lay frozen with fear. The others jerked their heads up at the same time and locked on Ben's position. They all extended accusing, bony fingers.

Ben gripped the sides of the narrow wall, trying to keep from falling. The world spun crazily as he lowered his hand to his side, grabbed the Battlerang from his back pocket, and threw it down in the direction of the creatures with all of his strength.

*AIIIIIEEEEE!* A loud sound like the feedback of one hundred microphones split the air. Ben grabbed his ears and hazarded a glance below. One of the creatures had fallen, its arm sliced neatly off by the blazing force of his lucky throw. The other guards leaped into action, rushing toward Ben.

Without wasting a moment, Ben dashed along the top of the wall, making his way to a low window on the side of the Presidential Tower. He was dimly aware of the other guards in the courtyard below sniffing the air as he ran past.

*CRASH!* Ben hurtled through the window in the Presidential Tower and fell to the floor a few feet below. Feeling dazed, he rose and quickly surveyed the hallway in which he now found himself.

Ben could never remember a time when the tower wasn't bustling with activity. Now the cubicles that lined the walls were strangely silent. As Ben furtively dashed in the direction of the stairway leading to Candlewick's office, a shadow at the end of the hallway caught his attention. He ducked behind the polished walnut wall of a nearby cubicle and watched as a familiar shape swung into view.

A dragon! And not just any dragon—this one was pink

with silver eyes. The beast emitted a long, low growl as it craned its head back and forth, scanning the corridor.

Ben's mind flashed back to several years ago, to the summer that his cousin had spent with his family. It was then that Ben realized:

*I know that dragon.*

The memory was still vivid in his mind. How in the world had a creature from Penelope's disturbed imagination come to Wishworks? Ben had hardly any time to contemplate the question when suddenly a booming voice echoed all around him.

"He's hiding in that office over there. Paddy, have the Horrible Snifters bring him to me at once!"

The next thing Ben knew, a black-cloaked guard was standing in front of him, its featureless face just inches from his own. Ben crashed to the floor, and then everything went black.

# ≋ Chapter Fourteen ≋

## President Penelope Piff

*T*he room swam into focus as Ben opened his eyes and tried to make sense of his new surroundings. Lacy pink curtains fluttered gently on the sides of a cracked sugar window. The walls sparkled with pink frosting and dripped with long vanilla icicles. Ben groggily lifted his head and noticed that the floor of the candy room was made of polished, purple flagstones. Something about the room was familiar . . .

Suddenly, with a rush of horror, Ben realized where he was. Candlewick's office had undergone a terrible change!

He tore his eyes away from the floor and over to where the brass elephant had once stood. Instead of the amazing Flooper Fizz dispenser, there was now a pink-taffeta-covered table with a ceramic tea set perched daintily upon it!

Ben's heart skipped a beat as his eyes flicked to the center of the room. Penelope's guards, the Horrible Snifters, were lined up against the pink walls, standing at attention. Where Candlewick's carved walnut desk had once been, there was now a glittering throne of rock candy and lollipops. Sweetums, the giant pink dragon, was sleeping, curled about the throne's base. Ben slowly lifted his gaze to the person on the throne.

Sitting lazily, with one leg dangling over the arm of the chair and a diamond tiara perched on her head, was Ben's dreaded cousin, Penelope Pauline Piff.

"YOU!" Ben gasped. Penelope yawned and glanced out the cracked sugar window, pretending that she hadn't heard him.

"Glad to see me?" She turned back to Ben and smiled evilly. "When I found out that you, dear cousin, were living in such an amazing place"—she nodded at the garishly decorated walls and ceiling—"I just had to come and pay you a visit."

"Penelope, where's Thom?" Ben demanded.

"It doesn't matter. I run this place now. You can call me 'my queen' from now on. I don't like my underlings to use my first name."

Ben felt his face grow hot with rage. "Penelope, tell me what you've done with Thom!"

Penelope scowled at Ben. "I told you not to call me that anymore." Ben watched as she removed a hot pink nail file and began to work on her stubby fingers. "Your friend Candlestick, or whatever his name was, is gone. I don't know where he is." She glanced up at Ben and scowled. "Doesn't really matter. I'm the only one who's important around here now, aren't I? After all, it was *my* birthday wish[14]!"

Ben stared at his cousin, putting two and two together. "So you made a *wish* to be president of Wishworks? But, how could you know about this place—"

Ben was interrupted by a reedy voice with an Irish accent that sounded from behind Penelope's throne.

"With a little help from yours truly." A leprechaun wearing a pink bowler and bow tie approached the side of Penelope's glittering chair. He folded his arms and smirked. "The name's Paddy O'Doyle. Wishworks needed some new

---

[14] If Penelope had confessed the specifics of her wish, according to the wishing rules it would have been canceled immediately. Unfortunately for Ben, she was clever enough not to have made such an obvious blunder.

leadership. I myself have taken over as the new manager of Kids' Birthday Wishes Ages 3 to 12. Your old job, I believe?"

Penelope giggled. "Paddy has made a few changes, helped improve things a lot." She addressed the little man. "Why don't we show Ben what we've been up to?"

"I think that would be appropriate." Paddy turned to the Snifters and shouted. "LIGHTS!"

The lights in the room dimmed and a very large monitor rose from behind Penelope's throne. Familiar images of children visualizing their birthday wishes appeared on the screen.

The first boy, who Ben thought couldn't have been more than six, was poised over the dancing flames of his birthday candles and visualizing a race car set. After he blew out the candles, there was a knock at the front door. Excitedly, he rushed to the door and greeted the brown-suited delivery man, who handed him a large package.

Grinning broadly, the small boy unwrapped the paper. His expression suddenly changed. Ben watched with horror as the boy screamed and dropped the box that contained not a race car set, but instead a twelve-foot-long hissing python!

Image after image flickered on the giant screen, revealing scenes of similar tragedies. A girl who wished for a pony was terrified when she found a saber-toothed tiger in her backyard, snapping hungrily at the family's little dog. A boy made a wish for a new video game and, when he reached into the box, cried out with disgust as he pulled out a handful of smelly dog poop. Countless images of birthday wishes around the world that had gone horribly wrong flashed in front of Ben's eyes, each worse than the last. Finally the awful images stopped and the lights came back up. Penelope, looking very satisfied, spoke.

"Nice work, Paddy; a major improvement."

The evil leprechaun smiled and tipped his hat at Penelope. After several moments, Ben finally found his voice.

"It's not possible. The Factory can't make wishes into curses. The machines wouldn't be able to—"

"Actually, that is where you're wrong, young man." The cloaked form of Rottenjaw emerged from the shadows, interrupting Ben. "With a few modifications supplied by Curseworks, the wish-generating machinery has proven quite adept at making curses." Rottenjaw tilted his head at Penelope. "All *she* had to do was supply the power source."

Rottenjaw held up an ornately designed lamp. The attorney raised a gloved hand and rubbed the side of it in a quick motion. A wisp of blue smoke emerged from the lamp's spout, then a defeated-looking Jinn bound with translucent chains materialized in the center of the room.

"What is your wish, o my master?" the Jinn said flatly, his voice barely rising above a whisper.

"NO!" Ben shouted. He couldn't believe what he was seeing! Penelope had actually imprisoned a Jinn in a lamp! His stomach turned as he gazed at the helpless creature.

Rottenjaw adjusted his small glasses with an imperceptible smile. "When Mr. O'Doyle arrived here last night, he wasted no time informing Mr. Thornblood that Wishworks was interested in a corporate merger with Curseworks. Your cousin is the president, and Adolfus Thornblood is her new vice president and business partner. As you can see"—he waved a black leather glove to indicate the Snifter guards standing at attention around the walls of the throne room— "your cousin's proficient imagination has already proved a benefit to both parties. When Thornblood arrives with his Curse-atina, I think he will be very pleased."

Ben stared at the balding attorney, his eyes narrowed with hatred.

"I should have known that your boss was behind all this."

Then, turning his attention to Penny, Ben said, "I don't know what you did to Thom." His voice caught in his throat, overcome by emotion. "But I can't let you do this to the Factory. It's not right!"

Ben's eyes burned with tears of frustration. He never had the chance to apologize to Candlewick, to make right the argument they'd had the previous day. He hated Penelope for taking him away, for removing the last and only parental figure in his life.

Penelope cast a baleful eye on her cousin. "Sorry, Ben. This is *my* factory now, and thanks to my Jinn, I can do anything I want with it."

Penelope rose from her throne and walked over to a nearby balcony. She pointed dramatically at the needlelike spire of the Feathered Funicula and ordered the captured Jinn into service.

"I wish you'd destroy that thing. Make it into something more to my liking."

The Jinn bowed low and said, "Your second wish, o my master, I hear and obey." Ben ran to the balcony, pleading for the Jinn to stop. But the Jinn was bound by magical law[15] to obey his master's orders.

With a flash of smoke and a burst of green fire, it was done.

---

[15] Once a command is given to a Jinn by its master, it cannot be changed. Very few Jinns are magically powerful enough to resist such a command, but there are rare and exceptional cases where ancient Jinns of great magical ability had the power to refuse.

The tower full of flying chairs was suddenly transformed into a huge birdcage filled with fluttering pink vultures.

Penelope chuckled as she strode back to her throne. Ben walked to the balcony and clenched his fists in helpless rage. The Feathered Funicula was the symbol of the Factory. He could remember staring at the machine in wonder, amazed by its delicate beauty as he walked to work every morning.

Now it was gone forever.

"Guards, take Ben to the dungeon. I want him locked up."

The Horrible Snifters saluted their queen, then sniffed Ben out and hobbled in his direction. Ben desperately scanned the balcony, seeking an escape route. His fingers groped for the Battlerang he kept in his back pocket, but found nothing. He realized with a sinking feeling that Penelope must have taken his weapon while he was passed out.

"Ben! Down here!"

Ben dashed over to the railing and saw Gene, hovering on a trail of smoke with his arms outstretched. The Jinn's face was earnest. "Jump!"

The Snifters were close and Ben knew that it was his only chance. Closing his eyes tightly and praying that Gene wouldn't miss, he swung his legs over the railing and leaped into the air.

"NO!" Penelope shrieked as he fell.

Ben crashed into Gene's strong arms with a loud *thud*. Gene quickly lowered them both to the ground and the two raced across the courtyard, leaving bewildered Snifter guards in their wake. They tore through an open door at the far corner of the terrace and disappeared.

"Don't let them get away!" Penelope screeched from the balcony. The sightless guards sniffed the air for a moment, catching the elusive scent before hobbling after them as fast as they could go. Penelope clenched her fists, her face purple with rage. Wheeling around to address her captive Jinn, she shouted, "Do something!"

The Jinn shrugged its massive shoulders and said, "What is your wish, o my master?"

Penelope's face darkened. "Find them!"

The Jinn nodded his head slowly, then, with a burst of crimson fire, the magical creature shot off through the opened window to search for the fleeing prey.

# ≈ CHAPTER FIFTEEN ≈

*Escape!*

"Quick, follow me! I know a shortcut!" Ben and Gene raced down a winding stone passageway. Emerging moments later inside the Fulfillment department, Ben raced with Gene to the brass door that he and Candlewick had been through earlier. Ben stuffed his hand into his jeans pocket and pulled out the key that Candlewick had given him.

*I only hope this door is as invulnerable as Thom said it was.*

Suddenly, a crashing noise pulled the boys' attention from the lock. A door burst open at the other end of the room, and a dozen Horrible Snifters now flooded inside, their noses sniffing in their direction.

"Go!" Ben shouted as he pulled the heavy brass door open. The two boys dashed inside, slamming the big door quickly behind them.

The Snifters wailed as they threw themselves against the barrier, unable to penetrate the magic door.

"That was really close," Gene said, wiping a purple hand across his sweating brow.

"How did you know where I was?" Ben asked.

"Jonathan told me you went after Candlewick. I figured you would be in his office." Gene nodded toward the door, looking concerned. "Can those things get through?"

Ben shook his head. "I don't think so. Thom said that that door is supposed to be invincible." He glanced at it worriedly. "I hope he's right."

After a few tense minutes of listening to the pounding on the door, the two were relieved to hear that the Snifters couldn't get through.

Exhaling softly with relief, Ben glanced over at the cement pillar that held the Cornucopia. He figured that it had been a couple of hours since he had run into Jonathan at the Thaumaturgic Cardioscope. He silently hoped that Perkins and the others were still waiting for them inside.

Gene's eyes boggled as he gazed at the incredible

submarine for the first time. The awestruck Jinn's mouth hung open as he followed Ben to the long ladder that extended from the ship's deck. Moments later, Ben led Gene down the hatch and into sub's richly apportioned interior.

"Ben! I was so worried!"

Nora's face was filled with relief as she spotted Ben and threw her tiny arms around his leg in a fierce hug. After releasing him she gazed up at him sternly. "Jonathan told me you ran off. What were you thinking?"

Ben shrugged and looked despondent. "I thought Thom was trapped. I had no idea what I was in for."

The round form of Perkins emerged from the room behind them, followed by Jonathan Pickles. "Tell us what happened."

Ben related the full story to the rest of the group. Perkins nodded worriedly as Ben told them about his cousin Penelope and all of the damage she had done. Nora and Jonathan looked sick when Ben mentioned the birthday wishes that had been turned into curses, and Gene was outraged when he heard about the imprisoned Jinn.

"But I thought that all of the magic lamps were destroyed!" he exclaimed with his fists clenched. "It shouldn't be possible!"

Perkins adjusted his bifocals and replied awkwardly.

"Well, yes, the problem remains that the Factory records are a little vague on that point. Nobody ever knew if they were actually destroyed or just had been cleverly hidden somewhere." The rotund man shrugged his shoulders. "I never thought that it would happen again[16]." He paused with a troubled expression. "Thom would be outraged if he knew that a Jinn had been imprisoned."

Nora looked distraught. "She's got to be stopped. All those poor, unhappy kids out there who are getting terrible things for their birthdays . . ."

"But I don't get it. How did your cousin figure out how to capture a Jinn in the first place?" Jonathan asked, puzzled.

Ben replied, "There was this evil-looking leprechaun named Paddy O'Doyle who took the credit for getting her up here. Maybe he gave her the idea."

Nora gasped with shock. "Paddy O'Doyle! But, that's my uncle!"

---

[16] The last time a Jinn was imprisoned was in 1972, when Shirley Sommerfeld, a resident of Tacoma, Washington, found a Jinn lamp at a garage sale. Mistakenly thinking it was an unusual watering can, she polished the lamp with brass polish and was surprised when the suddenly smoking lamp revealed a very displeased Jinn in her living room! It took the Wishworks Factory over a month to sort out the problem, and Ms. Sommerfeld only agreed to release the Jinn after being promised a wish. The neighbors remarked on the changes to her husband, Herb, for many years afterward.

# ⪧ Chapter Sixteen ⪦

## The Secret Mission

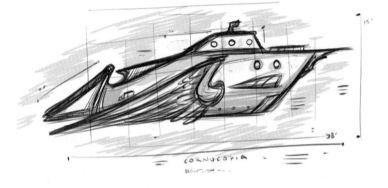

CORNUCOPIA

The others turned to look at the astonished leprechaun. "He used to work as a watchmaker in my parents' clock shop. They fired him because he was caught stealing from Wishworks when he made his deliveries to important Factory executives." Nora looked grim. "He was banished. Mr. Candlewick found out that he was supplying Curseworks with some of our family secrets. He forced Paddy to leave the wish dimension and live on Earth."

"I bet he must have one of the magic watches with him," Ben surmised. "That's probably how he got my cousin up here."

A buzzing alarm interrupted the conversation. The four followed Perkins as he rushed into the cockpit of the submarine and checked the control panel. Out of a slot in the brass console, a white paper emerged displaying information in old-fashioned type. Perkins studied the paper before looking up with a grim expression.

"It's a report from Warren, Wallace, and Wimbledon[17]. I sent them to keep tabs on everything going on inside the Factory. The Jinns found out that Penelope has one of their number imprisoned in a lamp." He paused before continuing, running a troubled hand across his forehead. "As of ten minutes ago, all of the Jinns in the Factory have gone on strike and fled, returning to the Jinn Territories."

The group listened to the news in stunned silence. Ben noticed that Gene seemed especially troubled by the news, his usual healthy purple color turning a shade of green. Finally Jonathan spoke. "So, without the Jinns' magic, Wishworks has no power. If we can't get the wish-fulfilling machines going again, the Factory will be ruined!" His eyes were round with fear.

Perkins corrected him. "*Limited* power." The older man

---

[17] The incredible clockwork spies for the Wishworks Factory.

did some quick calculations in his head before continuing. "There is probably enough residual magic to keep the Factory running for a while. For a couple of days, anyway." Perkins sighed. "It doesn't leave us much time."

Ben felt like he couldn't breathe. It was amazing how quickly everything had gone from bad to worse!

"So what now?" Nora asked. "You said you had a plan."

Perkins straightened. "I do."

He opened a wooden cabinet and took out a roll of parchment. "As of right now, I've rounded up all of the employees still loyal to Wishworks in a secret underground room. They are getting ready for battle. My job will be to keep Penelope occupied with the Wishworks Army while the four of you complete some very important tasks."

Perkins laid the parchment flat on a table, revealing a large blueprint of the submarine.

"The first part of the plan involves you two." Perkins indicated Gene and Jonathan. "The Cornucopia is much more than it appears to be," he said mysteriously. "During the First Wishworks War it was one of four magical weapons designed by President Finneas Cheeseweasle to defend the Factory[18].

---

[18] The other three weapons' hiding places were never discovered, and only vague descriptions still exist of the "Thumper," the "Impeacher" and the "Whirling Whizzy."

It was damaged in the war, but I think it's possible to repair it. The wings that are stowed in the engine room below look like they will still work."

Ben interrupted. "Wings? This thing can fly?"

Perkins nodded. "At one time it could fly faster and farther than any Feathered Funicula chair, and it could shoot magical torpedoes of devastating power."

Jonathan interrupted, looking excited. "A secret weapon?" He rubbed his hands together eagerly. "Can I get a look in the engine room? I'd love to get down there and start working on it."

Perkins rolled up the blueprints and handed them to him. "With your mechanical knowledge and Gene's piloting skills, I'm counting on you getting her repaired and in the air as soon as possible."

The two boys looked determined and wasted no time in going belowdecks, eager to get started.

"You mentioned *four* weapons. If the Cornucopia is one, where are the other three?" Ben asked.

Perkins shook his head. "Only Thom would know. We need him now more than ever. Thom once told me that if the Jinns ever went on strike, he had a secret backup plan that would save the Factory." He looked seriously at Ben and Nora. "But that's where you two come in. Have either of you heard of Thaddeus Snooplewhoop?"

Nora looked curious. "Yeah, sure. You mean the guy that ran Snooplewhoop's Everlasting Circus?"

Perkins looked at her questioningly. "Do you know where it's located?"

Nora grinned. "Of course I do. Went there every year when I was growing up. It's famous all over Leprechaun County."

Perkins nodded. "Well, I don't know if you remember your Wishworks Factory history or not, but he was president during the sixteenth century."

"Wait! I read about him," Ben said excitedly. "When a president ends his term, he's granted a single wish. Thaddeus Snooplewhoop wished to live forever[19] and created an Elixir of Life, but died in a trapeze accident, right?"

Perkins smiled. "Not exactly. That's the official story. The truth is, however, that rumored 'accident' never happened."

Candlewick's assistant folded his arms across his chest. "Thaddeus Snooplewhoop worked out an agreement with his successor, Socho Rumbleroot, to keep his wish secret.

---

[19] The wish for immortality is considered by the few that have successfully made it to be overrated. The major complaints are as follows: First, that *forever* is a lot longer than the people ever imagined. And second, that there aren't enough restaurants with special *senior* senior citizen's discount menus for people over two thousand and fifty-five.

They invented the story to keep other people from making the same wish and recorded the trapeze-accident story in *Wishworks Presidents, Past to Present.* Then, the story spread. It had to be that way. A wish like that could have created all kinds of problems on a larger scale."

"Wow, and I thought all this time that it was Snooplewhoop's great-great-great-grandson who was running the circus," Nora said, awestruck.

Perkins gave them both a serious look. "Well, you can't breathe the truth to another soul. I need your promise."

Ben and Nora nodded seriously. After a stern glance of approval, Perkins continued. "Snooplewhoop is the only living Wishworks president who would know what happens when a president of the Factory is wished out of power. If anybody knows where Thom has gone, it's Thaddeus Snooplewhoop. You two are going to have to find him and ask for his help."

Nora looked thoughtful. "That's going to be tough. Penelope destroyed all of the Funicula chairs. Leprechaun County is at least a week's hike from here. If there's only enough magic to keep the Factory going for one or two days, we'll never make it in time."

"She didn't destroy *all* of the chairs." Perkins looked uncomfortable. "I only wish that we didn't have to use the one chair that's left."

# ≋ CHAPTER SEVENTEEN ≋

## The Channel Five News Report

"**G**ood evening, I'm Libby Sanchez, and welcome to the Channel Five News at Seven." The anchorwoman's face was drawn and intense.

"In our top story tonight, reports are coming in from around the world about the growing epidemic of birthday party disasters. Children everywhere are receiving dangerous and sometimes disgusting birthday presents. We now go live to our reporter Peter Sinclair, who is at the birthday party of eight-year-old Charles Benchley in Simi Valley, California. Peter?"

"Thank you, Libby." Peter Sinclair, a tall, skinny reporter with red hair, stood next a large house that was swarming with exterminators. The camera followed him as he moved over to the anxious parents of Charles Benchley.

"If you could, Mr. and Mrs. Benchley, please describe what just happened at your son's party."

The reporter placed the large microphone in front of Mrs. Benchley, who took it with a trembling hand.

"We had planned Charlie's party for weeks. He wanted a new dump truck—he even circled the exact one that he was hoping for in the catalog." She took a deep breath. "I . . . I don't know what happened. When he unwrapped the present we had bought him, those *things* came out!"

Peter spoke into the microphone. "Could you tell us exactly what they were?"

"Horrible creatures. They attacked my poor son!"

Mr. Benchley's eyes suddenly grew round and he quickly pointed to an area behind the reporter's back.

"Look out! There're some of them now!"

A troop of big green-and-red-striped tarantulas came rushing around the corner of the house and let out an otherworldly screech. The largest spotted a pack of frightened exterminators and bared its dripping fangs. The exterminators panicked and dropped their supplies, running for the safety of their trucks as the spiders thundered after them, plowing deep furrows in the Benchleys' front lawn as they tore after their prey.

The reporter turned back to the camera. "Um . . . I better get out of here. Back to you, Libby."

Libby Sanchez turned her view from the monitor back to the camera. "Thanks, Peter."

She groped nervously for one of the scattered papers on her desk. "Similar reports are coming in from everywhere. Strange monsters are roaming the streets. Brightly wrapped packages containing deadly contents are appearing from nowhere. The president has issued a general warning, instructing all citizens to avoid unwrapping any gifts of any kind until the military can figure out who is behind this sinister plot.

"People are advised to stay inside and lock their doors. There is no knowing where the unexpected attacks might strike next."

Suddenly a commotion in the newsroom erupted behind the cameramen. Libby Sanchez screamed and dove under her desk as a ten-foot-tall, pink, two-headed gorilla smashed one of the cameras and rushed for the desk she had been sitting behind. With a beastly roar, the creature let loose a mighty swing and crashed its fists down upon the desk, shattering it into smithereens and revealing a petrified Libby Sanchez curled up beneath it. Before the woman had time to register what was happening, the ape grabbed her around the waist and hoisted her upon his shoulder as he leaped out of a nearby window.

Several papers fluttered down amidst the debris that had once been the newsroom desk. The shouts and screams of the television crew filled the air. A panicked voice yelled, "Cut to a commercial!"

The screens of television sets across the country flickered to black, and the seven o'clock news report was replaced by the happy jingle of a Doggie Munchies advertisement.

# ≈ Chapter Eighteen ≈
## Old Number Thirteen

**B**en gazed down at the dusty chair with apprehension. Written in scratched, flowing letters around the bottom half of the dilapidated machine were the words Lucky Penny 13.

"Old number thirteen[20]," Perkins said reluctantly. "It was the only number not allowed in the Lucky Pennies

---

[20] Old number thirteen was responsible for over 126 crashes during the First Wishworks War. President Cheeseweasle ordered it grounded in 1913, and the chair was considered so unlucky that most Funicula pilots have refused to touch it ever since, worried that any contact with the vehicle might transfer the bad luck to themselves.

Squadron. Unfortunately, this chair's had more bad luck than any other."

Ben examined the chair, noticing the tremendous amount of wear it had sustained. Most of the control knobs were broken, and one of its wings hung limply to the side with most of its feathers missing.

It looked like a disaster waiting to happen.

"Are you sure that this is the only one left?" Nora asked Perkins nervously. Ben knew that he and Nora shared a common fear of flying.

Ben had pretty much conquered his fear of flying during the last war when he had served as a Battlerang gunner, but the thought of going up in such a rickety chair made him nervous.

"If what Ben told us about Penelope turning the Funicula into a big birdcage is true, then I'm afraid so."

Ben gazed back at the door.

"How do we fly out of here?" he asked nervously, comparing the size of the doorway to the big chair.

Perkins indicated a switch on the wall. "The ceiling opens up. You should have a clear shot to the Factory walls from here." The portly man scratched his cheek. "I'm sure that Penelope and her guards will be watching for any sign of escape. Go as fast as you can to the south and try for as much altitude as you can manage."

Ben adjusted his big top hat, pressing it firmly down on his head. Nora found a gear bag nearby and discovered two rusty Battlerangs. Ben gratefully accepted the one she tossed to him and placed it in his hip pocket, hoping that the weapon still worked.

Nora climbed onto the armrest next to the pilot's controls, and as Ben was about to board he felt Perkins's gentle hand on his shoulder.

"I know you and Thom argued yesterday. Thom felt badly about it." Perkins hesitated before continuing. "He thinks the world of you, Ben. Never forget that. He was just worried about you."

Ben felt relief spread from his head to his toes. He smiled back at Perkins and gave him a quick hug before stepping into the flying chair. In spite of the danger of the mission and the unlucky chair that he was about to fly, Ben was full of hope. Candlewick was out there somewhere, and he was going to go find him.

Ben grabbed the control stick and nodded for Perkins to open the ceiling. Perkins threw the switch and the heavy roof doors slid open slowly, revealing the cloudless night sky.

"Contact!" Ben shouted as the ancient wings of the chair flapped to life. Perkins shielded his eyes from the dust clouds as the feathered chair rose into the air and climbed upward out of the small room.

"Good luck," Perkins whispered as Ben and Nora flapped out of sight and into the starry sky.

# CHAPTER NINETEEN

## A Perilous Flight

The wildly flapping Funicula chair ascended with increasing speed. Ben hazarded a look down and saw several Horrible Snifters crouched low to the ground, sniffing outside of the Fulfillment building like hounds that had lost track of their prey. He crossed his fingers, silently hoping that they didn't catch his scent up in the air.

After a few tense minutes, the twinkling lights of the Factory receded behind them and Ben allowed himself to breathe. The Snifters hadn't smelled them, and it seemed as if their escape would go unnoticed.

Sinking back into the soft, striped cushions of the flying chair, he sighed, staring at the mass of stars and shadow that sprawled in front of him. The wind was crisp as the chair sped through the night, bearing the scent of the pine forest that stretched endlessly beneath them. In any other circumstances, flying a Funicula chair at night might have been an enjoyable adventure.

"Ben, what's that glowing thing on the right?"

Ben turned and looked where Nora was pointing. A dimly lit object seemed to be moving in the same direction as they were. Ben couldn't make out what it was, but it was gaining on them with increasing rapidity.

Ben eased the throttle switch forward, accelerating the chair. Whatever the thing was, he didn't want it to catch up. The ancient chair lurched forward with its wings flapping frantically. Nora shouted over the beating feathers, her voice anxious. "It's still coming, Ben. Go faster!"

"I'm trying!" Ben shouted, urging the chair forward. The throttle was pushed all the way to the maximum drive setting. Ben searched the control panel for any switch that might make the chair go faster, but he couldn't see anything.

Suddenly, a jet of hot purple light shot over the back of the chair, nearly blinding them with its intensity. Ben reacted immediately, swerving the flying machine into a deep dive and out of the rays of light.

"It's Penelope's Jinn!" Nora bellowed, her hair flapping wildly in the wind. "It's trying to shoot us down!"

Ben's hands gripped the control stick and he tried not to think about his churning stomach as he pulled back hard, forcing the chair into a steep climb.

As they rocketed skyward, Ben caught a momentary glimpse of the Jinn's ghostly outline, still following closely behind them. Two more jets of magical energy burst from the Jinn's outstretched palms, and seconds later Ben's heart skipped a beat as he heard one of them smash into the side of the chair with a sickening *CRUNCH!*

In an explosion of splintered wood, the ancient chair lurched to the side and spun out of control. Ben's heart thudded wildly as he felt the flying machine plummet to the earth.

"Hang on!" Ben shouted as the chair spiraled downward. The ground rushed upward in a dizzying motion. Ben knew that if he didn't act soon, it would be all over—few Funicula pilots were able to pull the chairs out of a deadly spin.

*Stay awake, stay awake!* Darkness threatened to overwhelm his vision and he gritted his teeth, fighting the impulse to black out. Ben was dimly aware of Nora's panicked screams beside him and knew that the ground must be getting close.

Although Ben didn't have a lot of experience flying (he preferred to act as Battlerang gunner instead), training with a gifted pilot like Gene had taught him a few things. Suddenly remembering the Jinn's instructions, Ben whipped the control stick into the direction the chair was spinning and then jerked hard to the left.

*GROOOAAAN!* The flapping wings strained in response. Ben could hear tree branches scrape the bottom of the chair as it struggled to regain altitude. When Ben thought his arms would burst from the pressure of pulling on the control stick, the ancient chair stopped the deadly dive and pulled out, the ground just ten feet below. If it had taken a few seconds more, they would have crashed!

"Take the stick!" Ben shouted to a stunned Nora, who stared back with a blank expression.

"WHAT?"

"Take the stick!" Ben reached into his back pocket and produced the rusty Battlerang. Nora, catching on, nodded and moved to the pilot's controls. Ben stood on the cushion of the chair and gripped the armrest with one hand, his weapon with the other.

The Jinn was nowhere to be seen. Ben scanned the night sky for several minutes, but couldn't see any sign of their pursuer.

Suddenly a bolt of purple magic blasted down from above, narrowly missing Ben's head. Nora yelped and turned the chair to the left as Ben whirled toward the source of the blast.

"I see him!" Ben shouted. "Level off so I can get a good shot!"

Nora leveled the chair as Ben reared back, preparing to throw. The Jinn was slightly out of range.

*Wait for it . . . wait for it . . .*

The unsuspecting Jinn sped closer, the palms of his hands beginning to glow with power. At this range, the next magical blast couldn't miss.

*Just a few more feet . . . NOW!*

Ben hurled the Battlerang with all of his might. Fortunately the rusted weapon still worked, and burst into white fire as it whistled toward its target in a deadly arc.

*AIIIIEEEEEE!* The surprised creature's eyes widened as the weapon made contact. Seconds later the Jinn was gone, dissolving into wisps of gently shining smoke. Ben's heart sunk as he watched him vanish. If there had been any other choice, he would have taken it.

Sinking back into the chair, he wiped the sweat from his forehead. For a long while neither of them spoke, each silently grateful that their lives had somehow been spared.

After a while, Nora broke the silence.

"Do you think the Jinn was glad it happened?" she asked quietly.

Ben thought a moment before replying. "I don't know. I hope so."

Nora eased the chair a little higher, soaring comfortably out of range of the towering trees. Ben stroked the arm of the chair and gazed at the dilapidated flying machine with affection.

"You know what?" Ben asked.

"What?"

He hazarded a small smile. "Maybe this old chair isn't so unlucky after all."

# CHAPTER TWENTY

## *Thornblood*

"**B**e careful with that, fools! It's priceless!" The four Spider Monkeys carrying the heavy instrument on their backs tried to keep it from tipping. Thornblood placed his hand on the edge of his Curse-atina, guiding it carefully past the stone columns that lined the entryway to Penelope's ornate palace.

Thornblood eyed the palatial decorations, the latest in Penelope's wish list, with contempt. The palace had taken the place of the President's Tower and was decorated in typical Penelope fashion. Pink and purple furniture sprawled in every direction, and sickeningly sweet tapestries of teddy bears and ponies hung from the walls.

"So, this is my new business partner?" Penelope's voice rang out from her throne, an even bigger version of the one she'd had before. She chewed on a long rope of red licorice as she addressed the Curseworks president with a critical expression. "You're really weird looking."

Thornblood bristled, his skull-like features tightening at the insult. If it wasn't for the fact that the girl controlled the Jinn he needed, he would have commanded his Spider Monkeys to finish her where she sat.

Controlling his rage, he bowed stiffly. "Your majesty has a way with words." Penelope snorted and continued to chomp on her candy.

"Yeah, well. I call 'em like I see 'em," she drawled. "So, tell me, Thornbutt, what's with the big piano?"

"Why you little brat . . ."

Thornblood hissed and lunged toward Penelope's throne with his cane raised threateningly. Rottenjaw, trying to avert a disaster, dashed from Penelope's side and leaped in front of the raging president. "What Mr. Thornblood *meant* to say was that the item in question is not a piano, but something of far greater use to your majesty." Rottenjaw held back the sputtering president and motioned for the Spider Monkeys to bring the Curse-atina forward.

Penelope gazed at the dark machine, enthralled with its finger-bone keys and skull-shaped pipes.

"What does it do?"

Rottenjaw explained. "It's a device capable of converting wishes into curses—very special types of curses, m'lady. Curses of such frightening proportion that they almost destroyed Wishworks in the last war." Thornblood, having recovered his composure, pushed the simpering attorney out of the way and stared haughtily at Penelope.

"It would have succeeded, if it hadn't been for that cousin of yours." Thornblood noticed Penelope's expression grow irritated at the mention of Benjamin Piff. Adjusting his tall stovepipe hat, he continued smoothly. "With this machine we can be sure to achieve victory over whatever the Wishworks Army could throw at us. I'm sure that even now, Thomas Candlewick's assistant is plotting against us. It's only a matter of time before he launches an assault."

Penelope looked annoyed. "I'm not worried. I have a Jinn and I've got hundreds of *them*." She waved a bored hand at the rows of Horrible Snifters that lined her chamber. Her expression softened. "And I've got one other very special someone . . ."

Penelope whistled as if she were calling a dog. Suddenly

the sound of heavy feet shook the immense room, and then the huge form of Sweetums slunk into view from a side chamber. The dragon yawned hugely, exposing rows of vicious-looking teeth.

"Oh, my baby-waby!" Penelope cooed. "Did my wittle sweetie-peetie have a nice sleep? You did, didn't you . . ."

The huge dragon didn't respond, but slunk to its spot at the bottom of Penelope's throne and closed its silver eyes. Penelope looked lovingly at the dragon before turning her gaze back to Thornblood.

"You see? I'm ready for anything they could throw at me."

Thornblood's looked ill, the effect of listening to the singsong voice Penelope used to address Sweetums. After taking a moment to regain his composure, he responded.

"Let me assure you, Miss Piff, the Wishworks Army has a lot of tricks up its sleeve. Besides, with my weapon, once you have finished off their army, you can turn it on the people of Earth." The Curseworks president's expression grew hungry, relishing the prospect. "Just imagine the possibilities. If you have any enemies at all, my Curse-atina will torture them with curses that they will never forget. This is far greater than the alterations you've made to your wish-making machinery here in the Factory so far."

Penelope gazed at the instrument. After a long moment of consideration she commanded, "Show me how it works!"

"It requires the use of your Jinn, my queen. May I have the lamp?"

Penelope nodded regally as Rottenjaw approached the throne and removed the golden lamp from its nearby stand. The attorney handed it to Thornblood, who placed it into a custom-made holder on the Curse-atina.

Removing a sheet of handwritten music from his black coat, Thornblood sat on the bench and proceeded to play.

*SQUAWK! SCREECH! BRAAAAAP!* Thornblood stopped pressing the bony keys and looked up at Rottenjaw, confused by the instrument's sound.

"Maybe you need to rub the lamp first. That's what I always do," Penelope responded.

Thornblood grasped the lamp and began to rub furiously on its golden surface.

Nothing happened.

Rottenjaw moved over to inspect the lamp, peering inside its long spout. After a long moment he looked up at Penelope, his eyebrows knitted in concern. "Did the Jinn return after your last command?"

Penelope thought for a moment. "Let's see. I sent him after Ben and Gene. He returned to tell me that they were hidden in some kind of magic-proof room." She counted on her fingers, remembering the order of events. "I told him to patrol the area and wait until they came out. But first I wished for my new palace, more Snifter guards, and some cheesecake." She looked up, puzzled. "I haven't seen him since."

Thornblood's face darkened with rage. Striding up the rock-candy stairs of Penelope's throne, he shook the iron head of his cane in her face. "You mean to tell me you've *lost* him?"

Penelope paled, looking genuinely afraid. "I . . . I . . ." she stuttered.

Suddenly the sound of trumpets split the air. Glancing out the opened window, Thornblood saw the golden banners of the Wishworks Army marching toward Penelope's palace. Drums rolled like thunder and helmets flashed in the morning sunlight.

Thornblood wheeled on Rottenjaw.

"Gather my remaining Spider Monkeys and get these . . . *things* into some kind of order!" He indicated the rows of Horrible Snifters with the tip of his cane. "I'm not going to let Wishworks escape my grasp once more!"

Rottenjaw leaped into action, calling for the Snifter commander to follow him, his black cape billowing as he exited the chamber. The Spider Monkeys that had helped Thornblood bring his Curse-atina into the room scuttled out the window, rushing to alert their fellow troops.

"And as for you . . ." Thornblood turned on Penelope, who looked terrified. "Without your Jinn, you are of little use to me. You might be president of this Factory, but you will take all of your orders from me from now on!"

Penelope nodded, not daring to oppose the intimidating figure. Thornblood strode to the open window and gazed down upon the ranks of his soldiers gathering in the courtyard. He smiled grimly, noting how many there were.

*More than enough,* he said to himself. *This time I'll crush them for good.*

# ≋ CHAPTER TWENTY-ONE ≋

## Crash Landing!

"**D**o something!" Ben was awoken by Nora's terrified shout. His eyes snapped open and he saw the tiny leprechaun struggling with the chair's controls. They had flown for several hours and he had fallen asleep, lulled by the thrumming of the chair's gently flapping wings.

Now fully awake, Ben hazarded a terrified glance at the rapidly ascending earth. "Oh no! Not again!"

Ben squeezed in beside Nora and tried to pull back on the control stick, but it didn't budge. It had somehow become lodged forward in the down position and was forcing the chair into a steep dive.

"I don't know what happened!" Nora exclaimed. "One minute we were going along fine, and then the stick suddenly threw itself forward!"

The unlucky chair continued its fall, and in spite of Ben's heroic effort, no amount of tugging and straining would release the control stick. *It's the curse of number thirteen!* he thought with alarm.

Ben's life flashed in front of his eyes. *Not now! We've got to find Thom!*

Suddenly Nora shouted in Ben's ear, pointing at an especially large green field at the edge of the woods. "Aim for that field!"

"Why?" Ben shouted back, wrestling with the controls.

"Just trust me! Do it!" she commanded. Ben responded by trying to edge the stick to the right. He pushed with all of his might and the chair slowly responded, still locked in its downward descent.

The dark green patch of field loomed closer, rushing into view with tremendous speed.

"Brace for impact!" Ben shouted as the chair rushed toward the earth. He shut his eyes and gripped the arms of the chair. *This is really it!* he thought as the ground rushed inevitably forward.

"FIVE . . . FOUR . . . THREE . . . TWO . . . !"

Ben was dimly aware of Nora's shouts, counting down the seconds to impact.

*Here it comes!* he thought, his heart racing with terror.

# ≈ CHAPTER TWENTY-TWO ≈

## Lucky Clover

**B**ut just when the earth-shattering *KABOOM* should have happened, the chair inexplicably came to a gliding stop, and gently hovered a few inches above the green grass.

Ben opened his eyes.

The wings of the chair were tattered and unusable, but folded neatly at the chair's sides as if it had made a perfect landing.

He glanced at Nora, whose eyes were still closed and her knuckles white around the armrest of the chair.

Ben gazed around in disbelief. It was impossible!

He shook Nora and said, "Look! We're okay!"

The two opened their eyes and looked down, amazed.

"It worked," she said, and grinned. Nora jumped out of the chair and started whooping and hollering with uncontrollable fervor. "I knew it! It's clover! Four leaf clover! Watch!" She vaulted herself backward into the field of shamrocks and instead of crashing to the ground, hovered gently above the tiny plants on a magical cushion of air, completely unhurt.

Ben stared at her, openmouthed. Nora got up and took him by the hand. "There's nothing in the world luckier than a field of four leaf clover!" She grinned as she helped Ben to the ground. "It must have canceled out number thirteen's curse!"

Ben felt the springy turf beneath his sneakers. It was almost like he wasn't wearing any shoes at all! The powerful magic of the plants produced a warm, tingling sensation that he could feel in the soles of his feet.

Soon both of them were laughing and rolling about in the clover. No matter what happened next, good fortune was sure to be on their side.

Ben watched as Nora bent down and plucked one of the tiny stems and put the clover carefully in her breast pocket.

*"Gluais faicilleach le cupan làn."* She looked up and smiled

at Ben, who seemed confused.

"It's Gaelic, the old language of the fair folk. It means, 'Go carefully with a full cup.'" She patted her pocket. "Four leaf clovers are always lucky. But if a leprechaun uses one . . ." She grinned. "Let's just say that you're in for a dose of good fortune you'll never forget."

Ben smiled. Right now he felt like he could use all the luck they could get. He had a feeling that finding Candlewick wasn't going to be easy.

He and Nora stood up and turned in the direction of a mossy hill in front of them. Ben gazed at the green rolling landscape stretching in every direction.

"We better take the radio with us," Nora said, going back to the flying chair. She unclasped the receiver and handed it to Ben.

Ben noted that the gauge that measured the radio's battery power was full, and nodded with satisfaction. "Good idea. We can radio back to the Cornucopia and let them know when we've gotten to Snooplewhoop. By the way, how far are we from the circus? Can you tell where we've landed?"

Nora squinted at the surroundings for a moment before replying.

"Not a clue," she said simply, shrugging her shoulders. "Besides, the circus is always on the move. Our best bet is to find some locals and ask."

Ben and Nora headed toward a nearby hill. After about twenty minutes of walking they found a tiny dirt path that led them over the top. They had followed it for about fifty feet when suddenly Nora spotted a small white signpost that pointed to a left fork in the path.

"By Patrick's boots," she said under her breath and then turned to Ben, her eyes sparkling. "What did I tell ya? The luck's already begun."

Ben approached the carved sign and read the single word painted on it.

*SNOOPLEWHOOP*

# CHAPTER TWENTY-THREE

## Snooplewhoop's Everlasting Circus

*B*en marveled at the magnificent patchwork tent fluttering in the mid-morning breeze, surrounded by signs that promised a spectacle of incredible proportions. Following a long line of pint-size leprechauns into the tent, Ben ignored the many whispers as several recognized him as the Wishworks Factory's birthday wish manager.

Ben had been to the circus once when he was little, but the one he remembered didn't look anything like this! Strange, multi-armed fairies juggled balls of green fire, never missing a single throw. A beautiful mermaid crooned haunting songs while playing a harp. The crowds of leprechauns cheered as Finn MacCoul, a giant almost as tall as the highest tent pole, staged a mock battle with his archrival, Cuchullain. Ben thought that the second giant looked even fiercer than the first, with wild red hair and a beard that looked like tree roots.

As they edged their way through the crowd, Ben read the colorful signs that were posted at eye level for the leprechauns (about knee level for him): *Twenty-four hours a day! Seven days a week! Your father saw it. His father saw it. His great-great-great-great-great-grandfather saw it! Now it's your turn! See Snooplewhoop's Everlasting Circus! It'll be here long after you will!*

Several other signs explained the various attractions.

*Amazing! Astounding! Straight from the wishing well pipeline comes Grunchy Grubb, the gnomish bubble maker. Bubbles bigger than buildings!*

Ben smiled at the picture of the bearded gnome blowing a bubblegum bubble that looked as big as a house. He strolled to the next sign and read:

*Tatty McVarnish and his Irish floggers, Leprechaun County's crackyback experts. Watch as they hit targets up to ten miles away while blindfolded and hung upside down in a tank full of ferocious sea serpents!*

The sign showed a group of leprechauns wearing knickers and carrying tiny quivers filled with clubs of various sizes. He wondered if crackyback might be similar to golf.

He was about to examine the other signs when Nora waved Ben over to a door that said OFFICE and pulled him downward so that she could shout above the tremendous din.

"He's in there. You go ahead. I'm going to use the radio to check in with Gene and Jonathan."

Ben nodded and waved good-bye to Nora as he turned and stepped through the door.

Ben coughed as the spicy aroma of burning incense reached his nose. After his eyes adjusted to the dimly lit room, he noticed that the walls were draped like a huge, silken tent. Big colorful pillows were piled everywhere on the floor, with unusual items perched upon them like exhibits in a museum.

The first pillow he came to held a small golden key. A sign next to the key read:

*The magic key of Gee. Created in 1608 by the leprechaun locksmith Geepers McCracky. Can open any lock made of solid gold.*

Ben shook his head and grinned, wondering why anyone would make a lock out of gold. It seemed to him like most thieves would want to steal the lock instead of whatever it was that the lock was keeping secure. His curiosity piqued, he moved on to the next pillow. He was surprised to see that it held an odd assortment of shrunken heads. The card next to these read:

*Placed here by the Thaumaturgic Cartographers for safekeeping. Not for sale.*

Ben thought the shrivelled heads looked pretty creepy, so he decided to move on and see what other items were in the office. He had just stopped by a pillow that held a bottle of magic polish for Jinn lamps when he heard a wheezy voice behind him ask, "May I help you, son?"

Ben turned around to see a very short, fat, wrinkled old man with gray wispy hair that seemed to fly in all directions looking at him inquisitively over a pair of very thick bifocals.

"Are you Mr. Snooplewhoop?"

"Yes." The old man stared at Ben for a moment, and then pointed a quivering finger at him, saying, "Wait a minute. You're the new manager at Wishworks, aren't you?"

"Yeah," Ben said, feeling surprised.

Snooplewhoop tilted his head and studied Ben carefully. "What's the matter, son? Is something wrong?"

Ben nodded and described all that had happened at the Factory. When he got to the part about Penelope making a birthday wish that made her the president of Wishworks and causing Candlewick to disappear, the little man's eyes narrowed, his expression suddenly fierce.

"In all my years I've never seen it happen. Never! Why, I can't imagine a worse thing since the infamous term of Gimble Grimyfist[21]!"

Snooplewhoop was silent for a moment and then held up a finger indicating that Ben should stay where he was. The ancient man turned and marched into a back room hidden by a big curtain.

After a few moments he returned, holding a very dusty book.

Snooplewhoop stared at Ben, his eyes taking on a focused intensity. "This book was given to me by President Sephira Sparkletoe." Ben looked at the book with awe. He remembered studying about Sephira Sparkletoe in *Wishworks Presidents, Past and Present*. If he remembered correctly, the book he was now looking at had to be over 450 years old.

---

[21] Gimble Grimyfist (1526-1527), the worst president in Wishworks history, earned his name because of the rusty, maggot-infested gauntlet he found while digging in his backyard as a child. Supposedly he put it on at age twelve and determined soon thereafter to never take the horrible glove off, claiming that it made him more powerful than anyone could ever imagine. The reality was, the stench from the glove was the only truly powerful thing about him, and people everywhere would try to avoid the strange boy wherever he went.

The old man's eyes twinkled. "She was an amazing woman. A fairy, you know. She was very beautiful indeed." The old man's eyes glazed over at the memory before continuing. "Her main area of expertise was studying the magical rules that made Wishworks tick. Devoted her whole life to the subject."

Snooplewhoop reached out a trembling hand and leafed through the yellowed pages, muttering to himself. After a few seconds he stopped and, putting on an old-fashioned pair of spectacles, said, "Here it is, under Presidential Mishaps." He scanned the passage and then made a clucking sound. "Dear, dear. It looks like as if it was something that needed to be kept secret. See, she wrote it as a riddle." He held the book open for Ben to see. Looking down, Ben deciphered the spidery writing.

*If a president is taken by wishful means,*
*Here are the steps to find him again.*

*Let no mortal journey there except in crisis,*
*For the sleepers inside demand three prices.*

*First and foremost, a Stroke of Luck,*
*For without its fortune, you'll be surely stuck.*

*A Flash of Brilliance is number two.*
*Pfefferminz used it when his chairs first flew.*

*And for the third, the Heart that's True*
*Must pass a test, or split in two.*

*Then the one thus captured is free to go.*
*Heed the words of Sparkletoe.*


Snooplewhoop took the book back and shook his head. "I'm afraid I'm not going to be a whole lot of help on this one. I was never good at riddles." The old man sighed, studying the first line of the poem again.

Ben felt stumped. He had no idea where to begin.

"Does any part of it make sense at all?" he asked hopefully.

The old man gazed at the book with his bushy eyebrows knitted together. After a minute he suddenly brightened.

"Well, I might be wrong, but this first part . . ." He recited the first line of the poem. "I think she *might* be talking about the Halls of Sleep."

"Where is that?" Ben asked eagerly. Snooplewhoop walked over to his desk and pulled out a map of Leprechaun County. He motioned for Ben to join him, and pointed to a spot on the western side of the map. "Over here by McMurphy's Bay, hidden in the mountains in a cave. It is a sacred place, the place where all of the Wishworks presidents end up."

Ben looked alarmed. "A graveyard?"

Snooplewhoop chuckled. "No, not like you're thinking. It is a magical place where the presidents of the past lay sleeping, waiting for the day that they'll be called back into duty once more."

Ben's mind boggled as Snooplewhoop continued. "The Halls of Sleep are cared for by an incredibly powerful Jinn named Hoccus. He's the brother of the once mighty Abul-Cadabra. The two of them are the only Jinns in recorded history to use their real names."

Ben nodded. He'd heard of Abul-Cadabra, the fearsome Jinn that had used the Lamp of One Thousand Nightmares during the First Wishworks War. But he hadn't heard that he'd had a brother.

"Is Hoccus evil, like his brother was?"

Snooplewhoop shook his head. "We don't know much about him, other than that he's probably the most powerful Jinn alive today. The only reason he cares for the Halls of Sleep is because he made a promise to Wishworks's first president, Cornelius Bubbdouble, to do so. And a Jinn always keeps his word."

Snooplewhoop handed Ben Sparkletoe's ancient book. "I believe that when your cousin made her wish, Candlewick was transported to the Halls of Sleep. It's the most likely place he'd be." The old president paused thoughtfully before continuing.

"The riddle hints at many difficult obstacles to get there. Probably protection that was set in place by Bubbdouble in the very beginning." He looked earnestly into Ben's eyes. "Be careful, son. It could be dangerous."

Ben's face was filled with anxiety as he nodded and thanked Snooplewhoop. Then, to Ben's surprise, the old president's face split into a wide, gap-toothed grin. "Remember, son, the Wishworks Factory was built on hope. Keep that with you and you'll be all right."

Ben nodded and smiled, encouraged. Snooplewhoop detected the change and patted his shoulder. "Atta boy. That's the spirit." He looked around his office for a moment, then found a pair of keys lying on the edge of his desk. Taking them, he ushered Ben to the door.

"You're going to need transportation to get to McMurphy's Bay. And I have just the creatures for the job."

Ben followed Snooplewhoop outside and over to the exotic animal pens. Nora spotted Ben and ran forward.

"I spoke with Gene. He says that the Cornucopia is

coming along really well, even though most of the parts are old and rusted. They're working as fast as they can." Her face grew serious. "Perkins has engaged Penelope's troops. From what they told me, Thornblood is helping her and it doesn't look good. Wishworks has lost a lot of soldiers, and the Factory's power is running out. Perkins says that he thinks they might only have a few hours left."

Ben's expression turned grim. "We better hurry." He looked over at Snooplewhoop, who had opened a pen containing two horselike creatures. They were covered with green fur and had strange, braided horns coming out of their forehead.

"Quadracorns[22]!" Nora exclaimed. "I didn't know there were any left!" Ben watched as she moved toward the closest creature and stroked its green furry nose.

Snooplewhoop beamed. "Fastest thing on four legs." Ben watched as he patted the four-stemmed horn of the big

---

[22] The wonderful quadracorn is a gigantic beast that is only found in the mountainous regions of the Faerie Lands. They can grow up to twenty feet at the shoulder, but average around ten to twelve. Their braided horns, which are greatly prized by musicians, produce the rare ability to sound like an entire orchestra when blown and play different pieces of music automatically, depending on the age of the quadracorn when it was harvested. The killing of quadracorns was decreed illegal by Sephira Sparkletoe in 1520, and it has been a rare and protected species ever since.

animal. "I've even seen one outrun a Funicula chair."

"How fast can they get us to McMurphy's Bay?" Ben asked, feeling anxious to get started.

"If you leave now," he said, squinting at the sun, "I'd say you'd be there before dark."

Ben thanked Snooplewhoop as he climbed aboard one of the gentle beasts. The old man had to use a small ladder to help Nora aboard hers, and after he did so, he whispered something into the quadracorns' ears.

Suddenly the creature underneath Ben let out a wild neigh and shot from the pen, racing across the lush green fields at a terrific gallop. Ben clutched the quadracorn's flying mane and held on for dear life. He hazarded a look at the ground and saw it speed beneath the animal's hooves. In spite of the terrific speed at which he was traveling, only one thought echoed in his mind:

*I only hope it's fast enough.*

# CHAPTER TWENTY-FOUR

### The Siege

"**S**ir, permission to speak freely?" The young lieutenant's white and gold gauntlets sparkled as he saluted Perkins, his senior officer who was bent over a map of the Factory and studying it intently.

"Granted, lieutenant."

"We've lost over one thousand employees this morning." The young man looked anxious. "Thornblood's Spider Monkeys are bad enough, but our Battlerangs have to hit each of the Snifters at least five times before we can get through their armor." He ran a nervous hand through his blond hair.

"What I'm trying to say, sir, is that without Jinn magic at our disposal, we don't stand a chance!"

Perkins didn't look up from the map as he calmly addressed the sweating lieutenant. "And your idea on this matter is what, lieutenant?"

The young man licked his lips nervously. "All I'm saying is that if we launch a covert attack to take out the girl, maybe it will stop all this."

Perkins continued studying the map of the Factory. After a moment he placed a small, silver, W-shaped token on the map in front of the Factory gates.

"As I've said before, Penelope Piff cannot be removed from power unless she willingly unwishes her wish. No matter how powerful the magic that anyone could throw at the girl, there is a deeper magic behind all this that is much more powerful. A child's fulfilled wish is not something that can be easily undone."

The tired man raised his eyes and looked at the lieutenant. "Secondly, I don't think that it would help. Remember, Thornblood is up there commanding the troops. Penelope might be a novice, but the president of Curseworks isn't."

A look of panic crossed the young soldier's face. "But, sir, then that means there's no hope . . ."

Perkins smiled gently and his kind eyes twinkled as he

laid a firm hand on the young man's shoulder. "Listen . . . if there is one thing I've learned from working at this Factory for thirty years, it's that *hope* is the one thing we always have."

# CHAPTER TWENTY-FIVE
## McMurphy's Bay

*B*en and Nora dismounted just as the sun was setting over McMurphy's Bay. Ben scowled. The "bay" had to be the ugliest body of water he'd ever seen. Black oozing slime crept along its dirty surface, emitting a smell that reminded Ben of old tennis shoes.

Nora was studying the rhyme that Sephira Sparkletoe had written while the quadracorns grazed nearby in a patch of tall grass. It had been twenty minutes since they'd stopped, and neither of them had a clue what to do next.

"Okay, so the first part says that without a stroke of luck, we'll be surely stuck." Ben gazed at the putrid waters in front of him and scowled. "I feel stuck already." Nora grunted in agreement and stared out over the black water, searching for an idea.

"Where did Snooplewhoop say the cave was?"

"He didn't exactly say, only that it was near McMurphy's Bay," Ben replied, kicking a loose stone into the stagnant bog. The muck on the surface of the water was so thick that the stone actually sat on the surface for a few seconds before sinking down with a sickening slurping noise.

"Eww," Nora said, wrinkling her nose in disgust. "Have you ever smelled anything so vile—"

Her words were cut off by a sudden splashing noise emerging from the area where Ben had tossed the stone. Ben and Nora looked at each other with alarm. Something was moving beneath the surface.

"Look out!" Ben shouted as a great jet of spray shot up twenty feet, throwing mucky chunks of slime in every direction.

Seconds later the back of a huge black serpent roiled through the water, followed by a gruesome head with catfish-like whiskers.

"A sea serpent!" Nora shouted.

Ben and Nora nervously removed their rusted Battlerangs

and fell into fighting stances. Ben's heart pounded in his chest as the mammoth serpent[23] reared up in front of them and roared. They barely had time to react before it was suddenly barreling toward them at top speed, churning up a massive wake.

Ben steadied his nerves and focused on his target. "Ready, now!" Ben and Nora reared back and threw their Battlerangs in perfect, practiced unison. Months of Battlerang practice had taught them both the value of a double attack, typically increasing the damage.

*CLANG!* Nora's Battlerang glanced off of the serpent's scales just below its head, missing the mark. Ben's Battlerang collided with the horns of the beast and ricocheted harmlessly before returning to his hand.

"It's tough!" Ben mumbled anxiously as he fingered the still warm Battlerang. He was an expert with the weapon and had never seen one of his tosses do so little damage.

The sea serpent bellowed again, preparing to strike. Ben and Nora reared back for a second throw. Nora shouted, "Aim for its neck! Ready, set . . ."

---

[23] When St. Patrick made his legendary effort to banish all of the serpents from Ireland, a few of the bigger ones needed someplace to go. Scotland agreed to take one for Loch Ness, and the others forced their way into the Wishing World, much to the distress of the people that lived in Leprechaun County.

*SCREEEECH!* This time the howling monster was ready for the attacks and defended itself, easily ducking the speeding Battlerangs and using its snapping jaws to retaliate. Ben barely jumped aside in time to avoid one of the huge teeth that smashed down into the embankment, inches from his leg.

"What's with that thing?" Ben stood up shakily from where he had fallen. "It's like it can time our attacks!"

Nora nodded. "It's too heavily armored. We can't make a dent!"

The battle continued, the sea serpent seeming to have limitless strength. The monster wheeled and lashed, and at one point would have smashed Nora with one of its coils if Ben hadn't dived to her rescue.

"Thanks," Nora breathed as Ben helped the tiny leprechaun back up. Ben nodded and looked worriedly back at the towering serpent. Its long black neck was weaving back and forth like a cobra, and its eyes were fixed on Ben and Nora, contemplating its next strike.

Nora suddenly lit up with an idea. "Ben! The words in Sparkletoe's poem! A *stroke of luck!* I think I know what we need to do!"

She quickly reached into her pocket and grabbed the four leaf clover. Holding the small plant over Ben's Battlerang, she gently pressed the leaves together and whispered something in her people's ancient tongue.

*"Go gcuire Dia an t-ádh ort!"*

The two of them stared awestruck as tiny sparks fell from the clover's leaves and Ben's weapon glowed with a soft, light green light. Feeling hopeful, Ben grasped the weapon and marched to the churning water's edge.

The sea serpent fixed its gaze upon Ben and let out a loud screech. Ben reared his arm back, aiming with everything he had for the serpent's ugly head.

*FLASH!* Green fire burst from the spot where the lucky Battlerang struck the monster between the eyes. A horrible scream ripped from the creature's throat as it thrashed wildly before hurling itself back into the depths of the bay with a splash.

"You did it!" Nora grabbed Ben's leg in a wild embrace. Ben was almost knocked over from the impact and reached over to a nearby boulder to catch his balance.

A gentle ripple appeared in the water. Ben watched it, fearing the sea serpent's return.

Suddenly with a loud sucking noise, the water receded from the shoreline. He was reminded of water going down the drain in a bathtub as the bay grew more and more shallow, eventually revealing the sandbar beneath.

Nora gasped and pointed. "Look, there's a door in the sand!"

Ben looked where she was pointing and saw the large rusty-looking hatchway. The door was about thirty feet away and partially covered with weeds. "Come on!" he said excitedly.

"Wait, we should take the radio with us." Nora picked up the small box from where she'd left it near the quadracorns. Then the two made their way through the wet sand to the rusty hatchway.

Ben grasped the large iron ring in the center of the round door and pulled with all his strength. It creaked open to reveal a long, dark passageway.

Ben gazed into the tunnel apprehensively. It was pitch black inside.

"I wish I had a flashlight," he muttered, not liking the look of the dark passage. Suddenly the words of Sparkletoe's poem came back to him. *A Flash of Brilliance is number two. Pfefferminz used it when his chairs first flew.*

Ben smiled slowly, wondering if his idea might work. He turned to Nora. "The second verse of Sparkletoe's poem said that Pfefferminz used a flash of brilliance when his chairs flew."

Nora looked puzzled. "Who's Pfefferminz?"

"Wadsworth Pfefferminz was the second president of Wishworks and invented the Battlerang. In *Wishworks Presidents, Past to Present*, it also said that he was the first to employ Battlerang gunners in the Wishworks Army."

"He used a flash of brilliance when his chairs first flew." Nora gazed down into the dark tunnel. "Well, it sounds like it could mean a Battlerang. It's worth a try."

Ben took the Battlerang from his belt. It still glowed with the unearthly green luck that Nora had placed upon it. Aiming down the tunnel, he reared back and threw.

The Battlerang flew down into the darkness and disappeared.

After a few long moments, Nora turned to Ben and raised an eyebrow. Ben waited, holding his breath. It usually didn't take this long for a Battlerang to return.

A more few seconds passed.

Ben glanced at Nora and shrugged. "I guess it didn't work."

Nora nodded and pointed excitedly. "No, wait, yes it did! Look!"

The tunnel below them lit up with a ghostly green light, illumined by the glow of the returning Battlerang. As the spinning weapon made contact with the sconces that lined the cavern walls, green fire sputtered to life.

Ben grinned as he caught the returning weapon. "Cool!"

Nora smiled at him. "It looks like we've gotten through the first two lines of the poem. Now there's only number three."

She pulled out Sparkletoe's book and leafed through the pages. She read, *"And for the third, the Heart that's True must pass a test, or split in two. Then the one thus captured is free to go. Heed the words of Sparkletoe."*

Ben looked determinedly down into the tunnel's depth. The last part of Sparkletoe's rhyme sounded like it meant that Candlewick could go free.

Feeling buoyed by that hope, Ben lowered himself down onto the metal rungs. *Don't worry, Thom,* he thought. *I'm coming . . .*

## Penelope's Tantrum

"**I** hate him, hate him, HATE HIM!" Penelope beat the sides of Sweetums's scaly hide with her fists. The dragon took no notice, and continued dozing.

It had been several hours since Thornblood had assumed command of Wishworks, and Penelope hated the way Thornblood made her feel so scared and small. "It's my factory," she seethed. "He can't do this to me."

"Technically you're right, you know," Rottenjaw said, striding up to Penelope. "According to the wishing law, nobody can *make* you give up control of the Factory unless you willingly unwish the original wish you made."

"But he's so scary." She pouted. "Even my own guards won't listen to me anymore."

"I see your problem," the attorney said thoughtfully. "But there are other ways of getting what you want." Rottenjaw produced an important-looking document from his jacket pocket.

"This is the contract that officially merged Curseworks with Wishworks. Thornblood signed it, fully trusting that all of the fine print was in order." The attorney looked smug. "However, there were a couple of provisions that he didn't know about, a couple of well-placed words that I decided to add for good measure."

The attorney folded the document and replaced it inside his cloak pocket. "As of midnight tonight, the Curseworks Factory will require a new president."

Penelope looked up sharply. "And?"

"And, I think I know just the girl for the job," Rottenjaw continued smoothly. "If your majesty would want it, of course."

Penelope looked confused. "But I don't understand. If I can't stand up to him here, what would stop him from bossing me around over there?"

Rottenjaw's masklike face split into an uncharacteristic

smile. "There is one thing that Curseworks can offer you that Wishworks can't." He leaned forward. "There is a hidden magic buried deep within the Curseworks walls that can give you your power back. Thornblood knows that as long as a single stone of his factory is still standing, he retains that power." Rottenjaw stood up and adjusted his small glasses. "He is using it even now to intimidate the creatures he controls. To intimidate you."

Penelope considered the possibilities. Now that she had tasted power, she couldn't imagine giving it up. Ever since her Jinn had disappeared, she didn't have the ability to make her subjects afraid of her. She might be technically "in charge," but without the magical power to command, she felt useless.

She looked back up at Rottenjaw, feeling determined. "Okay, so what's the plan?"

"We wait until midnight." He examined his watch. "Then we head for Curseworks and you assume power."

Penelope stroked Sweetums's hide thoughtfully. "And what if Thornblood finds out?"

Rottenjaw snorted. "He won't. He's too busy exacting his revenge on the Wishworks Army. Let him try to get what he wants. Without Jinns to power this place, he's won nothing. Curseworks is the only place with any power left at all."

The attorney stared out the window, watching the two armies. The Wishworks Army, though smaller in size, was fighting fiercely to defend its home turf. A dozen Battlerangs sliced through the air, cutting through a troop of Spider Monkeys and Horrible Snifters. There was little doubt which army had the better warriors. The trained Battlerang troops attacked with orderly precision and refused to give up hope.

"Soon any residual magic that Wishworks has will be gone. Because there are no more Jinns in the Factory, their magical weapons will stop working and the resistance will fall apart." Rottenjaw scowled, watching the way the small army stubbornly resisted the Curseworks attack.

Penelope brushed a fringe of Sweetums's soft pink fur. "Well, now that I'm going to take over Curseworks, I don't want to lose any more of my new army than I have to." She gave her dragon an affectionate squeeze. "I think sweetie-peetie has had a nice nap and might like to go down and play now. Would you like that, sugar pie?"

The dragon yawned, exposing glittering rows of sharpened fangs. Penelope cooed and kissed it on the snout. She had not wanted to use Sweetums in battle. She had wanted him to be nice and hungry for when she captured Ben. But as the possible new president of Curseworks, she didn't want to lose any more of her subjects than she had to.

"Now don't eat too much of the Wishworks Army, honey pot," she said, tickling the dragon under its scaly chin. "Promise Mommy that you'll save room for dessert."

# CHAPTER TWENTY-SEVEN

## The Door

It seemed to Ben that he and Nora had been walking down the endlessly stretching corridor for hours, and he thought worriedly about how much time had passed since they had left Wishworks. Perkins said that the Factory's residual magic wouldn't last very long. He thought of his friends Jonathan and Gene and wondered if they had finished repairing the Cornucopia. Were they fighting Penelope's army of Horrible Snifters even now?

*If they can just hang on long enough for me to get to Thom . . .*

After several more minutes of walking, the end of the

corridor came into sight. At the end of the hallway were two ornate wooden doors. As they drew closer, Ben saw that they had names caved into each of them.

*"Benjamin Piff,"* he read on the taller door.

"By Patrick's boots." Nora whistled, looking at the smaller door with the name *Nora O'Doyle* carved onto it in sharp relief. "Looks like somebody knew we were coming."

"Yeah," Ben agreed, mystified by the doors. He felt anxious about what might be waiting for them on the other side. He gazed at his carved name and pulled his big top hat more firmly down on his head. Whatever waited was designed for them individually.

Ben reached into his back pocket for his Battlerang and glanced determinedly down at Nora. "Whatever this obstacle is, it's the last part of Sparkletoe's poem. If we can make it through this, we should find Thom."

Ben grasped the iron ring on the door in front of him with his free hand and took a deep breath. "On three?"

"On three," Nora agreed, grasping her own handle.

"Okay. One, two . . . three."

Ben's door swung open on noiseless hinges and revealed a pitch-black room inside. He walked slowly forward, feeling for any sign of a wall. The flickering light from the corridor behind him seemed to die in the shadow and revealed nothing but blackness in front of him.

"I can't see a thing in here, how's yours?" he called out to Nora. But before he heard her answer, the door suddenly slammed shut behind him, making the darkness complete.

Instinctively, he dashed back to where the door was, feeling for it blindly with outstretched hands. He had only walked inside the room a few feet and couldn't understand why his groping fingers couldn't make contact with the nearby walls. Moments later his hands brushed up against something different, something that didn't feel like a door at all.

Ben ran his hands alongside of what felt like a metal chair.

*What in the world?*

Continuing to inch his way forward, he felt a second chair placed immediately next to it, and then a third.

Suddenly the light in the darkened chamber changed, and rising all around him was a warm, incandescent glow. He wasn't inside the tunnel anymore. He stared around himself with disbelief, unable to process what he was seeing. It was impossible. It was a place that he had been in before, a place from back home.

*I'm in the Burbank Airport terminal.*

# CHAPTER TWENTY-EIGHT

## At the Cornucopia

"Arrrgh! Gene, give me a hand with this bolt, will ya? I can't budge it." Jonathan Pickles's exasperated, greasy face poked up from a hatchway in the submarine's deck.

"Coming!" Gene tore himself away from the yellowed manual that detailed the controls of the Cornucopia and rushed over to his friend's side. The area that surrounded Jonathan was littered with rusty parts, a jigsaw puzzle that looked impossible to put back together.

"Are you sure you can do this?" Gene asked skeptically as

he took the wrench from Jonathan.

"Yeah, I think so," Jonathan said. "Half of these parts are so corroded that I have to spend twenty minutes scraping off each one before I can put it back together."

The bolt that Gene was pulling on suddenly gave way under the Jinn's massive strength. "Got it." Gene handed the wrench back to the grateful Jonathan.

Suddenly the sound of quick footsteps echoed through the metal chamber. A haggard-looking Perkins poked his head inside the engine chamber.

"Are we close?" he asked hopefully.

Jonathan looked at the parts and nodded. "Getting there. I think I'll have it back together in another couple of hours. After that, it's anyone's guess as to whether it will actually start."

Perkins looked concerned. "What do you mean?"

Jonathan hesitated. "Well, when I traced the electrical system back to the control panel in the cockpit, I noticed something." The tall boy crawled out of the hatchway and wiped his hands on a greasy rag as he led Perkins and Gene to the front of the ship.

"See, right here. There's a part that's missing." Jonathan pointed at a shallow, circular depression in the console. "I'm thinking that whatever fits right there acts like an ignition key. I've searched the whole ship and haven't found anything that fits."

Perkins glanced sharply at Jonathan. "Can you get around it?"

Jonathan shrugged. "I'm going to try to hot-wire it, but I don't know. All I can do right now is get the engine in working order and then find out."

Gene spoke up. "I've studied the manuals, and if we can get it flying I'm sure that I can pilot it. It's not that much different from the 1955 Funicula Special Edition[24]."

Perkins nodded. "Good. I'm counting on you two."

"How are our troops holding up?" Gene asked.

Perkins sighed and adjusted the buckle on his immense breastplate. "Penelope's Horrible Snifters are tough to eliminate, sometimes taking three or four Battlerang hits to bring one of them down. Thornblood's Spider Monkeys are giving us the usual problems, but the troops are used to

---

[24] 1955 was an exceptional year for Funicula chair design, revealing such models as the McMurphy Thunderific and the Flapping Flash. The Special Edition, however, outshone them all and was a chair of incredible handling and unique design. Instead of the traditional two wings, it was equipped with four. The chair also had an aerodynamic, space-age design that was unrivaled, with chrome control sticks and big rocketlike fins. It was available in three colors: carnation pink, robin's egg blue, and putrid puce. The last color was the least popular.

dealing with them."

The elderly man looked grave. "But the biggest new problem is that dragon of hers. We've fired everything we have at it and it barely makes a dent. Without the Cornucopia's torpedoes, I don't think we will be able to stop it." Perkins adjusted his bifocals. "You boys need to have this thing in the air as soon as possible. I've ordered the troops to retreat to the spot where the Feathered Funicula once stood. That's where we will make our last stand."

Jonathan nodded grimly. "Then I'd better get back to work. I'll try every trick I know to get this thing started."

After Perkins left the room, the boys exchanged worried glances.

"Man, I hope Ben and Nora find Candlewick. He's the only one who can get us out of this mess," Gene said, picking up the ancient manual he had been studying and scanning it for any text he might have missed.

"Me too," called Jonathan from the grimy engine compartment. "And I hope he's got some good tricks up his sleeve." He grabbed a large mallet and took aim at an especially rusted lever. "We're gonna need them."

# CHAPTER TWENTY-NINE

### The Hardest Test

*I*n front of Ben was a busy place that looked exactly like the airport terminal back home.

*No way!*

He walked forward, inspecting the area. The seats he had felt in the darkness were placed in orderly rows next to a ticketing counter. It all felt way too familiar—it was exactly like the day he had been here with his parents, the day that he had said good-bye to them for the last time.

Right before the plane crash.

Ben walked to the end of the row of chairs and noticed

that there were three suitcases that looked very familiar.

"It can't be," he whispered as he spotted his own suitcase. His breath quickening, he inspected the luggage tags that he knew would be on the other two larger bags. Written in his mother's neat handwriting were his parents' names.

"Ben!" He wheeled around at the sound of the voice, a voice that he had heard in his dreams many times since the tragic event.

"Mom?" Ben stood frozen into place as he watched his mother, dressed in the same clothes that he remembered her wearing the last day that he saw her, rush toward him with tears running down her cheeks.

Moments later her arms were around him in a fierce embrace. Her familiar warm smell filled his nostrils as she drew him close. Ben reached up tentative hands to hug her back, his mind still reeling from the impossibility of what he was experiencing.

"Hi, Ben." A deep, gentle voice emerged from behind him. Ben's hands still gripped the folds of his mother's shirt as he turned to see his dad standing there, smiling at him like he used to so many times before.

Ben's eyes filled with tears as he felt his dad's arms around him. He felt the two people that he missed the most next to him once more, their strong reassuring arms giving him the comfort that he had craved for so long.

"How are you guys here? This is impossible," Ben choked out.

Ben's mother stroked his hair and smiled gently. "We've missed you, Ben."

Ben's dad smiled. "It's been too long since our family has been together, son. It's time for us to go home."

Ben stared up at his parents. They were really there. Alive. So perfect.

A worrisome thought, like a mosquito, buzzed in the back of his mind. *What if all of this isn't real?*

He looked at his mom, who playfully tugged on the top of his ear.

"Mom?" Ben began anxiously.

He struggled with what he was going to say next. He didn't want to cause this wonderful dream to vanish. But the voice inside of him pushed him to ask it anyway. He had to know.

"Mom, is this really happening?"

Ben's dad interrupted, tousling his hair. "Hey, what's it matter? The point is that we're here. Together as a family."

Ben's heart sank. His dad's blue eyes twinkled like they always did, but his words were the answer Ben had dreaded. Somehow what he was experiencing was some kind of

vivid dream.

The announcement came over the loudspeaker. "Flight 237 to Newbury Park, California, now boarding. All passengers to gate 21 for boarding, please."

"That's us." Ben's dad stood up and folded the magazine under his arm. Ben stood up next to his mother, his heart racing. He hesitated a moment as they moved toward the boarding gate. Should he really go with them?

His feet moving automatically and his mind racing, trying to justify what he was doing, he followed them to the door.

*Even if it's not real, I don't care,* Ben thought determinedly. *This is close enough. It's just as good as if they are really here. Dad's right. What does it matter, really?*

Then, just as they were about to pass through the door that led to the waiting aircraft, a voice called out from behind him.

"Hey, Ben, what about Wishworks?"

Ben spun around. Thomas Candlewick stood next to the ticketing counter, one elbow casually leaning on the attendant's desk as he examined his magical pocket watch like Ben had seen him do countless times before.

"Thom?"

The tall man looked up and offered Ben a small smile and a wave. Then, speaking kindly but intently, he said, "You shouldn't go, Ben."

Ben felt himself grow angry. He didn't want this moment to be ruined and would do anything to hang on to the illusion he was experiencing. He *needed* it to be real!

Turning his back on Candlewick, he forced himself to continue down the gently sloping ramp that led to the awaiting aircraft. After a few steps, Candlewick's insistent voice called out from behind him.

"It's a test, Ben, a test to find out if you are able to make peace with your past. It was set up to determine if you had what it takes to be a true Wishworks leader. You must choose wisely, even if the choice causes you pain." Candlewick's expression softened. "You can do it, Ben. It's hard, but I know that you can do it."

Ben felt a gentle tug on his hand. His mom's kind brown eyes looked down at him, full of love.

"Come on, son. We'll miss our flight."

The struggle inside of Ben at the moment was the worst that he had ever felt. The desire to board the airplane with his parents was overwhelming, and everything within him shouted that he should just ignore Candlewick and follow them.

But deep down inside of him, in a very small, secret place, he knew that Candlewick was telling him the truth.

He wanted this moment more than anything, but he knew that it wouldn't be the right choice.

He felt his mom tug on his hand again. Then once more, Candlewick's voice rang out.

"The Factory needs you, Ben."

*Don't listen. Just go with Mom and Dad. The people at Wishworks can take care of themselves.*

Ben was about to step onto the airplane, but couldn't help giving Candlewick one last look. The Wishworks president stood at the ticketing counter, watching Ben.

It hurt terribly to abandon the thing that he wanted most, but Ben knew that Candlewick was right. He couldn't leave his friends, or his responsibility to the millions of children around the world that needed hope.

"Mom?"

Ben's mother looked down at him quizzically.

"What is it, Ben?"

The words that Ben needed to say were harder than he ever could have imagined. His heart felt like lead and his lips were dry, and when he spoke, his voice was barely a whisper.

"I gotta go back, Mom."

Ben's mother stared at him for a moment and then knelt down beside him, looking into his eyes. She didn't say anything for a long time.

Finally, she kissed him on the cheek and looked deeply into his eyes.

"I'm proud of you, Ben."

Ben's eyes burned and he felt a warm tear roll down his cheek.

The airplane, hallway, and lights grew blurry and soon dimmed out of sight. The illusion vanished and Ben found himself back inside the darkened room, alone.

After a few moments, a small flickering candle emerged from the shadows. Ben watched as the person bearing the flame grew closer. It was a young girl about his own age with freckles and short, reddish hair. She was wearing an old-fashioned pilot's uniform with a beat up-leather aviation jacket. The birthday candle she held burned with a strong, steady light.

She approached Ben and stood in front of him for a long moment. She exuded a strength and confidence that Ben had never seen in somebody so young before.

The girl drew her face very close to Ben's own and stared deeply into his brown eyes with her bottle green ones. Ben felt a little self-conscious and hoped his eyes weren't still red and puffy from crying.

After a long moment, a satisfied look crossed the girl's

face. She cleared her throat loudly.

"I, Lucky Penny Thicklepick, recognize Benjamin Bartholomew Piff."

Another candle moved forward from Ben's left. A small boy, wearing the clothes of a medieval peasant, drew close, his pale, round face illuminated by his flickering flame. He, looked a bit younger than Penny, and where her face was full of courage, his seemed full of compassion and kindness. He, too, looked at Ben carefully for a moment before speaking in a soft voice.

"Ebenezer Hairyhead recognizes Benjamin Bartholomew Piff."

Soon there were other children, each bearing birthday candles, gathering around Ben. The light from so many small flames drove the darkness back and revealed that Ben wasn't standing in an empty cave any longer, but was instead in a tall, elegant chamber with beautifully crafted stained glass all around. He listened, awestruck, as each voice said a name.

"Wadsworth Pfefferminz recognizes Benjamin Bartholomew Piff."

The skinny boy dressed like a monk gave him a small smile.

"Sephira Sparkletoe recognizes Benjamin Bartholomew Piff."

A young fairy with bright blue eyes winked at him before walking away.

"Bertram Snicklepants recognizes Benjamin Bartholomew Piff."

Ben couldn't help smiling at the chubby kid with the cherubic grin, who held two candles and handed one to Ben.

"Thaddeus Snooplewhoop . . ."

Ben was surprised to see a much younger version of the Snooplewhoop he had met at the circus emerge from the shadows.

*They're all here,* he thought as each of the Wishworks presidents approached him, giving him their approval.

"Thomas Candlewick recognizes Benjamin Bartholomew Piff."

Ben turned to see a boy no more than two or three years older than he was with a longish chin and a blue derby hat. He gave Ben a younger version of the smile that Ben knew so well, and as he walked away, Ben noticed that he had two Battlerangs sticking out of the hip pockets of his jeans.

Soon all of the past presidents had gathered in a circle around him, some a little older than Ben and some a little younger, but all giving him a vote of approval.

All except one.

"I don't recognize him," a thin, reedy voice softly spoke from the back of the room. Ben watched as a tall, hawkish boy emerged from the shadows, handsome except for a long, purple, wormlike scar that ran down the side of his cheek. As he drew closer, Ben noticed that he wore a rusted gauntlet on one hand and refused to stand near the circle of flickering candle flames.

A puff of wind blew through the chamber, extinguishing all of the candles and plunging the room into darkness in one breath. There was a pause. Then, seconds later, Ben saw a heavy oak door open to his left, spilling white light into the chamber and revealing that the past presidents had disappeared.

Not knowing what else to do, Ben walked toward the blinding white light and stepped through the doorway and into whatever waited on the other side.

# CHAPTER THIRTY
### The Halls of Sleep

As soon as Ben walked into the stone antechamber, he was almost knocked over as Nora rushed over and grabbed his knees in a fierce embrace. "You passed the test!"

Ben glanced down at the little leprechaun. He thought of the last lines of Sparkletoe's poem, *And for the third, the Heart that's True / Must pass a test, or split in two.* Saying good-bye to his parents had been heartbreaking.

"Yeah, but that test was way tougher than I thought it would be," Ben said softly. "Have you found Thom?"

Nora shook her head. "I got here only a couple of minutes before you."

Ben looked around the immense chamber, searching for a clue as to what to do next. Towering marble columns rose around them on every side, supporting a roof that looked like it was inlaid with gold.

"Maybe there's something down there," he said, motioning for Nora to follow him. A large glass door was open at the end of the room.

As they drew closer, they saw that the door opened into a magnificent garden filled with exotic plants and flowers. Nora stopped beside a group of tall unusually shaped flowers with purple stems.

"Hogbottles," she said, intrigued by the plants. "Wow. They're really rare. People say that if you sniff one, all of your hair will fall out."

"I made that mistake once." Ben and Nora turned to see the oldest-looking Jinn they had ever seen approach, holding a bright red watering can in his hand. He had a silver beard that foamed over his chest like a waterfall, and eyes that were gray and reminded Ben of storm clouds.

"It took me over two months to find a magical antidote. As you can see, even with that, the hair on top never grew back." The old Jinn chuckled as he removed his massive turban and revealed his shining bald head underneath.

"You must be Hoccus," Ben said, remembering Snooplewhoop's description of the ancient Jinn.

The Jinn nodded and bowed. "At your service, Benjamin Piff." He straightened and indicated their surroundings. "What brings you to the Halls of Sleep?"

Nora piped up eagerly. "We're looking for Thomas Candlewick, sir. Is he here?"

Hoccus studied them both for a moment before answering. "The Halls welcome all employees who have served the Wishworks Factory well. I was notified that a new arrival was sent here recently under unusual circumstances."

Ben nodded excitedly. "That would be Thom. He was wished out of existence by my cousin, Penelope. She's taken over Wishworks and joined forces with Curseworks." Ben's voice turned desperate. "We have to find him—he's the only person who knows how to save the Factory!"

Hoccus stared at Ben intently, his brow furrowed with concern. "The Halls are a mysterious place. Those who come here to sleep are often changed. It might be difficult for you to recognize him."

"I don't understand. Is he still alive?"

Hoccus looked intently at Ben before answering. "I'll

show you what I mean."

The ancient Jinn removed a large silver key and walked over to a big door. It was made of intricately wrought silver with a quarter moon etched into its surface.

Hoccus pushed the door open to reveal a huge chamber filled with an endless array of unusual items. Stacked on shelves and crowding the floors were every kind of treasure imaginable. Golden light filled the chamber from tall windows, causing the rich array of items to wink and glitter beautifully.

"Wow," Nora said appreciatively.

"When someone enters the Halls, they are turned into an object that best represented them as mortals," Hoccus explained. The Jinn floated on a trail of silver smoke to a nearby shelf and removed a small golden bird figurine and handed it to Nora.

"Lucky Penny Thicklepick was known for her love of flying. She was never happier than when she was in the air."

Nora's eyes grew wide. The leprechaun stared down at the golden bird, hardly able to believe that she held the sleeping form of the thirteenth Wishworks president in her hands.

"Here, you better take this. I don't want to drop it," Nora said shakily and handed the statuette back to Hoccus. The

Jinn smiled gently and placed it back on the shelf.

Ben scanned the room, overwhelmed with the number of objects that met his gaze. "So all of these treasures represent employees that worked at the Factory?"

"Those that have done great service to the Factory," Hoccus said.

Ben surveyed the immense room. It was completely packed! How in the world would he ever be able to locate Thom among the countless gleaming artifacts?

He looked up at the Jinn, feeling desperate. "Can't you give me a clue to where he is? We don't have much time, and the fate of Wishworks is at stake!"

The Jinn slowly shook his massive head in apology. "I cannot. Only someone who knew Thomas Candlewick well can locate him." He stared at Ben. "Search your heart, Benjamin Piff. What item in this room best represents him?"

Ben tried to calm himself as his eyes flickered over the priceless paintings and fine jewelry, the golden candelabras, jeweled chests, and finely wrought silver cups. His glance fell on a silver-tipped cane that was carved with mythical creatures on its wooden shaft.

*That's not it.* There was nothing about the walking stick that resonated with Ben. Trusting that his instincts would guide him along, he took a deep breath and continued.

His gaze dropped to a small object resting on a low shelf in the corner of the room. *Could it be?*

Ben's hand tingled as he reached down to pick it up. It was so simple and yet so obvious that his face split into a wide grin.

"There you are," Ben whispered as he gently lifted the item. The golden pocket watch glowed softly in response.

"I've found him," Ben called over his shoulder.

Hoccus floated over and scrutinized the timepiece. After examining the watch for a moment, the Jinn turned to Ben and nodded in approval.

"You've done well, Benjamin Piff."

Nora looked up excitedly. "What do we do now?"

The old Jinn politely took the watch from Ben's outstretched hand.

Hoccus closed his eyes, bowed his head over the watch, and murmured a long string of incomprehensible Jinnish words. As the ancient Jinn spoke, Ben could feel the air around them slowly change as if it were charged with static electricity.

Hoccus's words must have been magical, because when Ben was handed back the timepiece, it glowed even more brightly.

The old Jinn smiled at Ben and said, "First you must picture him clearly in your mind. Then, after that, simply say his name and he will awake."

Ben glanced down at the watch's golden surface, trying to form a mental picture of Thomas Candlewick. His thumb traced the elegantly embossed initials *T.C.* on the cover, and he thought back to a moment long ago, when he had unwished his birthday wish for unlimited wishes. At that time, he had found himself immediately whisked back to his tattered cot at the horrible orphanage. It was like the wish had never happened, and he had been devastated.

Then Candlewick had shown up. Ben could picture him now, walking through the door and sitting down beside him on the small cot, putting a comforting arm around his shoulders. Candlewick had surprised him by inviting him to come up to live at Wishworks and become the new department manager. Where moments before Ben had thought his life was over, Candlewick had stepped in and given him hope. When he'd brought him up to the Factory and given him a home, it felt to Ben exactly like being adopted into a new family.

Ben smiled wistfully, picturing the moment clearly in his head. Gazing down at the elegant timepiece, he spoke softly.

"Thomas Candlewick."

The watch began to glow with a soft golden light. Ben laid the watch down on the flagstone floor and stood back as the glow grew brighter.

Then it happened. A shadowy form blurred into view and emerged from the golden light.

Ben joyfully beheld Candlewick's face, with its pointed nose and long chin, smiling back at him. His friend yawned and adjusted his blue derby. Then, after checking his pocket watch and snapping the cover back into place, he strode over to Ben and Nora, as if he had just woken up from a long nap.

Ben rushed over and embraced Candlewick in a fierce hug. Candlewick, caught off guard, almost toppled backward underneath the rush.

"Whoa! Good morning to you, too!" He smiled brightly and patted Ben on the back before glancing around at the cavern filled with treasure, looking confused.

"What in the world?" Then the Wishworks president looked over at Hoccus and his eyes grew wide with recognition. "Is it really you?"

The ancient Jinn smiled and nodded. "Welcome back, Thomas Candlewick. I hope you feel rested?"

Candlewick chuckled and shook his head, looking around in disbelief. "I actually do!" He whistled softly. "I

can't believe I'm inside the Halls of Sleep!" He gazed at the cluttered shelves lining the walls. "The last thing I remember, I was working late in my office when I felt this terrific pulling feeling, like I was being jerked right out of my chair."

"That was because my cousin, Penelope, made a wish to take over Wishworks," Ben put in.

He and Nora went on to hurriedly explain what had happened since Ben's cousin had made her evil wish. Candlewick listened attentively. When Ben finished the tale, Candlewick's face was pale and anxious.

"Well, it was a smart move by Perkins to try to repair the Cornucopia, but without my help it will never get off the ground." He looked worried. "By now the residual magic that powered Wishworks is probably almost gone. But if we hurry, we can still remove Penelope and Thornblood from power. We'll have to use the Impeacher."

"What's that?" asked Nora.

"It was a weapon designed by Cornelius Bubbdouble, the first Wishworks president, in case the Factory was ever taken over by evil forces. Only a person with the purest intentions for the Factory can use it. If anyone else tries to, the weapon will destroy them. We must confront Ben's cousin while holding the Impeacher and demand that she relinquish her claim on the Factory." Candlewick's face was grim. "If she does so willingly, her life will be spared. If she doesn't, she will be forcibly . . . *removed.*"

Candlewick paced. "We can get her out of power, but without the Jinns, the Factory will still be destroyed."

Candlewick's face suddenly lit up with an idea. He turned to Hoccus with a pleading expression. "I know that this has never been asked of you before, and I wouldn't ask it of you now except for the nature of this emergency. But, would you help us?" Candlewick stood in front of Hoccus with his hands outstretched.

The ancient Jinn's face grew very serious and Ben couldn't tell if Hoccus was angry or not. The Jinn stared at Candlewick for a long moment, before replying.

"I have sworn long ago not to be involved in the struggles of humans and my people. My brother felt differently and he perished for his cause[25]."

Candlewick seemed at a loss for words. He obviously hadn't expected such a blatant refusal.

Ben knew that the fate of Wishworks might hang in the balance, and that if he spoke up he might have a chance at persuading the Jinn to change his mind.

---

[25] Abul-Cadabra was supposedly destroyed in the First Wishworks War, although experts say that his body was never found.

He hesitated, feeling sudden waves of insecurity wash over him. He hadn't handled himself very well in the delicate negotiations with Rottenjaw. And not only that, hadn't Candlewick said that he doubted whether or not Ben was ready to be wish manager? Maybe it wasn't his place to speak up. Maybe he should just keep his mouth shut.

*Wise as a serpent, gentle as a dove.*

The words that Candlewick had spoken to him at the meeting with Rottenjaw came back to him. The saying applied now more than ever. Deciding to go ahead and say what was in his heart, Ben knew that this time he would phrase what he had to say with delicacy.

Mustering his courage, Ben approached Hoccus and said, "Sir, I know that you've said that you don't want to take sides. And I know that the relationship between humans and Jinns has been difficult." The old Jinn turned his intense stare on Ben. Ben tried to calm his rapidly beating heart and continued.

"But just because some bad humans imprisoned your people in lamps doesn't mean that all humans are evil."

Ben tried his best not to flinch under the Jinn's powerful gaze. It felt like staring into the middle of a thunderstorm.

"Cornelius Bubbdouble put his faith in you because you were the only one he could trust to take care of the Halls of

Sleep. He was a human and you decided to help him. I only ask that you would consider doing us the same favor. We'll respect whatever decision you make."

After a long moment, the Jinn spoke.

"I will consider what you have said, Benjamin Piff."

Then, without another word, Hoccus turned his back to Ben and floated to the heavy silver door and exited the room.

Candlewick turned to Ben and smiled. "Now *that* was well said. You've really given him something to think about." He glanced back at the silver door. "I really think we just might have a chance."

Candlewick punched Ben playfully in the arm and continued. "A birthday wish manager *and* a diplomat. I knew you had the right stuff. Reminds me a lot of myself at your age."

Ben adjusted his big top hat proudly. He could tell that the earlier argument was forgiven and forgotten. It was good to feel Candlewick's confidence in him once more.

Candlewick opened his pocket watch and, while twisting a dial to tune in to the location of the Wishworks Factory, said, "Okay you two, hang on. I don't know what we're going to find when we get to Wishworks." He pressed a button and the Halls of Sleep faded into blinding whiteness.

Although Ben desperately hoped that they weren't too late to save the Factory, he felt ready for anything. *Bring 'em on,* he thought. Now that Candlewick was back, they were halfway to victory.

# CHAPTER THIRTY-ONE
## The Impeacher

"**I** had no idea it would be this bad." Ben stared around at the wreckage in startled disbelief. Candlewick's pocket watch had transported them to the Pot o' Gold. All that was left now were scattered bricks and blasted tree stumps. Penelope's army had spared nothing in its attacks.

"Follow me." Candlewick's voice came in clipped tones as he led Ben and Nora purposefully through the remains. Abruptly, Candlewick stopped at a charred stump and knelt down.

"*T.C. and D.N.,*" Nora read, turning to Candlewick. "Did

you do this?"

Candlewick searched for something at the base of the stump's twisted roots. "Yep, when I was a kid."

Ben studied the initials and suddenly knew who D.N. might be. "So, you liked her even back then, huh?"

Candlewick cleared his throat. "I don't know what you mean," he said. Nora gave Ben a curious glance and Ben grinned, giving her an I'll-tell-you-later look.

Ben watched as Candlewick pressed a hidden switch underneath the stump's roots. The top of the table suddenly swung aside, revealing a secret storage area underneath.

Candlewick opened the elegantly carved box that was inside. Ben's heart leaped as he spotted several gleaming Battlerangs sitting on on a satin pillow.

"Wow, those are some 'rangs!"

Candlewick nodded. "I put these here for safekeeping. They are some of the original Battlerangs designed by Wadsworth Pfefferminz himself[26]." Candlewick distributed

---

[26] The second Wishworks president and inventor of the Battlerang. Although history states that it was born from a botched attempt at a heated backscratcher, the Battlerang has proved to be one of the most important weapons ever created. There are only a very few of Pfefferminz's original models in circulation and most have sold for exorbitant prices at Wishworks Factory auctions. There have been rumors that a couple of them were smuggled to Earth and ended up on eBay, but this is unconfirmed. An original can be identified by the inventor's signature on the bottom left-hand corner of the Battlerang.

two of the shiny weapons to Nora and Ben and then pocketed the last two himself. Ben stared at the gleaming surface of the perfectly balanced weapon. It was by far the most elegant Battlerang he'd ever held.

Candlewick dug deeper into the hollow stump and removed one last item that was wrapped in a velvet bag with golden tassels. "Here it is. The Impeacher," he said.

"Oh, and I almost forgot." Candlewick fished in his coat pocket for a moment and then handed an object to Ben.

"My watch!" Ben exclaimed as he eagerly took the timepiece from Candlewick and put it back on.

"I put it in my pocket after you left. I figured you'd still need it."

Ben smiled gratefully.

"So, what do we do now?" Nora asked anxiously. Candlewick held up his finger for a moment as he consulted his own watch. Ben glanced down at his, remembering how it had displayed a map that revealed where the Spider Monkeys had tunneled into the Factory. After watching Candlewick use his watch, Ben pressed the same button on the side of his own and a miniature map of Wishworks sprang into focus.

Red *X*s dotted the sprawling Factory's landscape, indicating where the bulk of Penelope's forces were. Ben's heart sank at the horde of enemies they would have to face and wondered if Perkins and the Wishworks Army were still okay.

"It doesn't look good," Ben said grimly, shaking his head.

Candlewick pressed several other buttons before replying. "It looks like Perkins has retreated to the Feathered Funicula."

"What once *was* the Feathered Funicula, anyway," Ben corrected, remembering the horrible transformation that Penelope had made.

Candlewick clipped his watch shut. "We don't have much time left, so we're going to have to split up." He handed the velvet bag to Ben, who took it carefully.

"I'm going to help Perkins resurrect the Cornucopia, while you two sneak into Penelope's throne room and use the Impeacher." He turned to Ben. "Set your watch coordinates for 7767. It will take you to a spot just outside her palace. The Impeacher demands that only a person with the best intentions for Wishworks use it. There is nobody I would trust with that responsibility more than you, Ben." Ben silently vowed not to bungle the mission like he had when he'd first gone solo.

Candlewick indicated the bag with a sharp nod. "Nobody should touch the Impeacher but you. Remember, if anybody with the slightest selfish desire to rule the Factory should take it, the ancient texts mention that there would be terrible consequences."

Ben wondered at the weapon's design. It felt as weighty as steel, but was also smaller and thinner than he had expected it to be.

Candlewick continued. "Now, everything I've read says that you are supposed to point it at the accused and say *J'dissh*, the Jinnish word for justice. The weapon was designed by a Jinn craftsman for President Bubbdouble. It looks like a judge's gavel, but it is filled with extremely powerful magic."

Ben nodded, feeling anxious. He hoped that Penelope would resign the presidency peacefully and not force him to use the weapon on her. Even though he didn't like her, he didn't actually want to cause her harm.

"Okay then. We'd better get started." Candlewick gave Ben and Nora and an encouraging smile. "Remember, Wishworks was built on hope. The battle isn't over yet. If you are successful in removing Penelope, there is a good chance that her army will give up."

Ben and Nora nodded, grateful for the president's encouraging words. Then, after setting his coordinates into his watch, Ben let Candlewick show him how to push the sequence of buttons to make his watch transport him and Nora to their destination.

Ben took a deep breath as he pushed the buttons and saw the corresponding bright flash of white light emerge from his watch. The last thing he saw was Candlewick's salute as he and Nora rushed off to face his dreaded cousin once more.

# CHAPTER THIRTY-TWO

## The Last Stand

"**T**ry it again." Jonathan touched two of the Cornucopia's coiled copper wires together, attempting to get the submarine to start.

"Nothing." Gene's defeated voice echoed back from the cockpit. He took his finger off of the ignition button and stared desperately at the machine's unresponsive gauges.

It had been over two hours since Perkins had left, and the boys had been working feverishly to get the Cornucopia to come to life. They both had the sickening feeling that Perkins and the Wishworks Army were fighting for their lives as they struggled to get the secret weapon to work.

"Well, I don't know what else to do," Jonathan's exasperated voice called from the engine room. "I've tried everything, but there doesn't seem to be any way to hot-wire this thing. Without the key, it just won't work."

Suddenly, a flash of light crackled through the inside of the sub and the two boys were startled by the arrival of Thomas Candlewick. He moved quickly to the console where Gene sat.

"Hi, guys. I hope she's ready."

"Mr. Candlewick! You're okay!"

Candlewick gave the massive Jinn a quick smile as he settled into the pilot's seat. "Yep, thanks to Ben and Nora."

"So they made it, too?" Gene sounded concerned.

Candlewick nodded. "They're going after Penelope as we speak. How's the progress on the Corn? Did you guys get her fixed?"

Jonathan wiped his greasy hands on a towel and called, "The engine should be in working order. Do you have the key?"

"Yep, right here." Then, to the boy's surprise, Candlewick removed his pocket watch and fitted it perfectly into the shallow circular depression in the ship's console, then thrust his finger at the ignition button. They all held their breath for a moment as they waited for the revving engine to catch. Then, to everyone's relief, the engine of the ancient vehicle sputtered and majestically roared to life.

"It sounds terrific!" Candlewick shouted above the engine's thundering roar. Glancing back at Jonathan he said, "You did a great job!"

Jonathan grinned and shouted back. "Thanks! It wasn't easy."

"I've already attached the wings. She should be ready to take off," Gene said.

"Excellent." Candlewick pulled another switch on the console labeled HANGAR DOORS. There was a loud rumbling sound as the ceiling opened, revealing the dusky night sky above.

"Have you studied the piloting manuals?" Candlewick asked Gene.

The Jinn nodded. "I've practically got them memorized."

Candlewick stood up and motioned for Gene to take the pilot's chair. "Good. She hasn't been flown since the First Wishworks War. It's going to be up to you to take her up." The Jinn nodded eagerly and assumed the controls. Seconds later the submarine's massive wings were a flapping blur as it slowly ascended into the sky under Gene's expert piloting skills.

After the winged submarine had gained sufficient altitude, Candlewick gazed below them at what remained of the glittering Wishworks Factory. From the vantage point of the Cornucopia, he could tell that many of the elegant buildings had been reduced to smoking ruin by the combined forces of Thornblood and Penelope. The damage was far more extensive than he had anticipated.

"Get us to where the Funicula tower used to be. Top speed!" Candlewick commanded.

"Roger," Gene replied, and pushed the throttle forward. The submarine responded smoothly and leaped forward, sweeping through the darkening sky like a massive shark in an ocean of stars.

"Hang on, Perkins," Candlewick muttered under his breath as they sped forward. "Help is on the way."

◎ ◎ ◎

The sun cast a reddish glow over the courtyard where the last of the Wishworks Army was assembled, preparing themselves for a final, desperate charge. Perkins scanned the faces of the few hundred Wishworks employees that remained, many of them with their arms in slings or limping from injuries. In spite of the overwhelming odds, the old man had lived his life never giving up, no matter how desperate the situation.

*There's always hope,* he reassured himself as he stared out over the cobblestone courtyard, waiting for the enemy troops to arrive.

Moments later the faint sound of beating drums reached his ears. A nervous wave of apprehension swept through the Wishworks Army. Perkins buckled on his golden helmet and walked to a clearing in front of his soldiers.

"Ladies and gentlemen!" Perkins's steady and encouraging voice quieted the rustle of anxious whispers. "This will be your finest hour." The portly man radiated assurance to his war-weary troops. "You have fought bravely, and I'm proud of each and every one of you. I know that we face an enemy that has superior numbers, and on the surface that seems daunting." A ripple of murmured assent swept through the soldiers. Perkins continued. "But hear me now. Although they might be many in number, each of you are worth ten of them in courage and skill."

The troops stared back at their leader, a flicker of hope crossing their anxious faces. Perkins strode to the front of the ragtag army and laid his hand on the shoulder of one of the men in front. The bearded man smiled at his leader. "I have lived and worked with each of you for many years. Jim here worked at the Falling Star department when I was the night shift manager more than twenty years ago."

The man nodded in agreement. Perkins patted him briefly on the arm before continuing. "Like each of you, Jim loved working here at Wishworks. Not just because it was a good job, but because he *believed* in what he was doing. *Believed* in the reason this Factory exists, isn't that right, Jim?"

"That's right, Perk," Jim replied, nodding vigorously. Perkins smiled at him before turning his eyes to the rest of the troops. "Each and every one of you feels the same. Without this incredible factory, there is no hope for mankind. We supply the dreams and hopes that keep people alive. That alone is worth fighting for, no matter what the odds."

A small cheer went up from the troops.

"So today, as we face a foe that wishes only to destroy, led by a leader who wishes nothing more than revenge and destruction, I tell you now"—Perkins fixed the army with a steely gaze—"we will not stand by and let them win. For they're not just fighting an army of dedicated Factory employees, but fighting against *hope* itself. And no matter what might happen . . ." Perkins's voice soared with confidence. *"Hope springs eternal!"*

A tremendous shout burst from the soldiers. Perkins grasped the arms of many of the men and women, igniting sparks of courage in each of their hearts.

Boom, boom, BOOOOOM! The war drums of Penelope's army were very close.

"Battlerangs ready!" Perkins commanded. The rasping sound of the glittering weapons leaving their sheaths swept through the ranks. At a nod from Perkins, one of the soldiers wound the cranks on the backs of Warren, Wallace, and Wimbledon, the robotic spies of the Wishworks Factory. The clockwork robots' eyes sparked to life and the triumphant strains of a bellows-driven bagpipe erupted from Wallace, signaling the ancient call to arms and heartening the Wishworks troops. Seconds later, the three robots had removed their spinning swords and were ready to be commanded into action.

Perkins's eyes narrowed as he viewed the troops of gibbering Spider Monkeys rushing forward, howling with demented glee. Several hundred Horrible Snifters followed the apelike monsters with their long white noses sniffing the ground, like hounds closing in on their captured prey.

"Steady! Wait for my command!" Perkins could feel his troops' anticipation building, like a tightened bowstring ready to fire. The whir of Warren, Wallace, and Wimbledon's blades whizzing like helicopter rotors was the only sound as the tension-filled army waited for their leader's command.

Gazing over the rushing horde of enemy troops, Perkins

saw Penelope's mammoth dragon suddenly charge to the front of the enemy forces, fire spouting from its nostrils in a deadly arc. Perkins waited until he could see the strange silver eyes of the beast and then shouted at the top of his lungs, "Ready, aim, FIRE!"

◎ ◎ ◎

Ben surveyed the spot where he and Nora had transported to, searching for any sign of Penelope's soldiers. The place Candlewick had sent them to just behind his cousin's massive palace looked deserted.

*So far so good,* Ben thought grimly. *Now to find a way inside.*

Ben scanned the low part of the wall that surrounded the palace for an opening. After a brief search, Nora spotted a stained-glass window a few feet off the ground.

To Ben's surprise, the window had been left unlocked. *Probably because she never expected the army to make it this far,* he reasoned. The window was just high enough for him to scrabble inside, but too tall for him to reach back down for Nora. Ben placed the velvet bag that held the Impeacher into his back pocket and hoisted himself upward into the abandoned room.

"You'll have to wait here," Ben whispered back down to Nora. "If I'm not back in an hour, you run and tell Thom, okay?"

Nora nodded, but seemed upset about not being able to go with him.

"You be careful!" she whispered. "Don't do anything foolish!"

Ben nodded, heartened by Nora's friendship and concern. Turning back inside the empty room, he spotted a spiral staircase leading upward. Hoping that it led to Penelope's throne room, he ascended, trying to keep the wooden steps from creaking as he climbed.

After a few minutes of climbing, he approached a small trapdoor. Ben could hear muffled voices coming from the chamber above and thought that one of them sounded a lot like his cousin's.

*This is it,* he thought. His heart pumped wildly as he gripped his Battlerang in a sweaty hand. Ben pressed his palms on the wooden door, inching it slowly upward so that he could get a peek inside the brightly lit chamber.

Penelope sat huddled in a corner of the room, terrified. A tall, skeletal figure stood towering over her. It was a figure that Ben recognized immediately as Adolfus Thornblood.

Without waiting another minute, Ben pushed hard against the door and sent it crashing open, hoping to catch his enemy by surprise. He leaped from the underground passage with a rush, skidding to a stop in front of the Curseworks president with his Battlerang poised to throw.

Thornblood wheeled around and spotted Ben.

"Benjamin Piff!" Thornblood scowled darkly. "Good to see you again." The Curseworks president drew a sword that was hidden inside his walking stick. "I would suggest you release your weapon and surrender."

Two Spider Monkey guards approached Ben, pointing their barbed spears threateningly. As Ben lowered the Battlerang and pretended to surrender, he felt with his left hand in his back pocket for the Impeacher.

Sudden dread rushed through him as he felt his empty pocket where the magic weapon had been. It was gone!

Thornblood caught the desperate searching look in Ben's eyes and spotted the bag lying on the floor by the trapdoor's opening at the same time Ben did.

Quick as lightning, Thornblood's Spider Monkeys scuttled to the entrance just as Ben leaped for the Impeacher. A sudden tug-of-war erupted between Ben and one of the creatures, both of them pulling hard on the velvet bag. Although Ben fought with all his might, the Spider Monkey was stronger, and moments later Ben felt the Impeacher slide out of his fingers.

"What's this?" The Curseworks president had a twisted smirk on his face as he reached a curious hand inside the bag.

Ben held his breath as he remembered Candlewick's warning about no one else touching the Impeacher.

Thornblood removed a small silver hammer from the velvet bag. He gazed at it curiously, inspecting its beautifully crafted surface.

Nothing magical happened.

Thornblood turned back to Ben with a curious expression on his face, obviously wondering why Ben had wanted the tiny hammer so desperately.

Suddenly, on an almost inaudible level, Ben was aware of a low hum. Slowly it began to build, a sound like the chanting of a thousand monks, reaching an ever louder thrumming crescendo. Thornblood stared around the large room, confused at the source of the sound. The humming chant grew louder and the Spider Monkeys reacted, writhing on the ground as if the low frequency was causing them immense pain.

As the sound filled the chamber, resonating from all four walls, Ben noticed that the light in the room had dimmed. Then Ben saw several familiar figures materialize in the room. This time they were not children like he had seen before, nor were they the objects he had seen in the Halls of Sleep. This time they appeared to be at the age they were in their presidential prime, as leaders of the Wishworks Factory.

Thornblood's jaw hung open as he surveyed the apparitions, unable to comprehend what he was seeing. Several Spider Monkeys shrieked and rushed from the chamber, terrified.

Ben watched as one by one, each of the apparitions turned toward the Curseworks president. All of the blood drained from Thornblood's face as he gazed at the assembly facing him.

Suddenly a howling wind rushed through the chamber. Thornblood gasped as wisps of ghostly energy surrounded his body, rotating around him in slow, deliberate circles.

He gave Ben a desperate look. "Call them off, Piff! We can deal . . ."

But before the words had left his mouth, the Curseworks president screamed with agony as one of the ghostly strands flew into his body. Moments later, bright energy surrounded him, driving him to his knees. He raised a hand to his face, examining it with horror as it began to bubble and smoke.

Ben watched transfixed as the president fell to the floor, writhing and screaming as whatever was inside of him devoured him from the inside out.

The still, white faces of the Wishworks presidents observed the punishment without expression.

Moments later there was nothing left but an echo as

Thornblood dissolved into powder, leaving no evidence that he was ever there except for his ebony-handled walking stick and the small silver hammer that lay abandoned on the floor.

◉ ◉ ◉

Down on the battlefield, Perkins and the Wishworks Army fought to hold their ground against the swarms of enemy troops. For every one of the horrible monsters that fell, ten seemed to take their place. Perkins had fought his way to the front, leading the charge against the most formidable of their opponents, the slithering pink dragon.

*Boy, am I gonna be sore in the morning,* the aging assistant thought as he parried and slashed with his glittering rapier against the snapping jaws of the beast. The fight was more of a workout than the portly man had had in a long time, but his inner courage fueled his aching muscles, forcing him onward.

*Left, left, right, spin, parry . . . thrust!* he thought, mechanically forcing himself through the training drills that he had practiced over the years. In his youth he had actually been fencing champion at Wishworks, a prestigious position held by only a few before him[27].

---

[27] Pierre de Chaumpinon, the famous Factory employee who attempted to fly to the moon in a Funicula chair, first developed the prestigious title of fencing champion. To earn the title, the swordsman must have defeated fifty enemies attacking at once without a obtaining a single scratch.

The dragon lunged forward, overextending its reach and snapping an area just right of where Perkins stood. Seizing the opportunity, he noticed a vulnerable spot and sent a precise stab into a soft area underneath the dragon's foreleg. The beast howled with rage and pain, spouting angry crimson bursts of fire from its nostrils as it reared backward.

"Bull's-eye!" Perkins shouted as he watched the dragon recoil. A nearby group of soldiers shouted in support as they fought through a crowd of Spider Monkeys.

Perkins had readied himself for a second attack when, unexpectedly, the beast whipped its barbed tail forward, sweeping in a deadly arc at Perkins's exposed side.

*CRASH!* The sound of the blow echoed through the battlefield as Perkins's body smashed to the ground under the impact of the forceful blow. The dragon let out a roar of triumph and stomped its heavy claws as the fighting momentarily stopped, a stunned silence descending on both armies. Perkins's inert form lay still and silent on the cobblestone street. The Wishworks Army stared, unbelieving at the inconceivable tragedy.

Thomas Candlewick's brave and stalwart assistant was dead.

Suddenly realizing that the leader of the opposing army had been defeated, a triumphant howl of victory burst from the lips of the combined forces of Penelope and Thornblood's armies as they anticipated the victory that was sure to come.

The Spider Monkeys and Snifters rushed forward into the stunned Wishworks troops, ravenous and grinning. Suddenly a shout from one of the soldiers erupted from the surging throng of monsters.

"LOOK!"

Flapping into view, its long golden wings outstretched in a rushing dive, was one of the four ancient weapons of the Wishworks Factory. The golden submarine banked to the left and took aim at the gigantic pink dragon, which stared uncomprehendingly at its new foe.

*WHOOOSH!* A torpedo propelled by crackling green magic erupted from the hull of the majestic ship. Seconds later it made impact, a direct hit into the scaly flanks of Penelope's dragon.

*BOOOOM!* The ground shook and several soldiers from both armies fell to the ground under the force of the explosion.

Seconds later, the dust and smoke cleared to reveal an incredible sight. Where the dragon had once stood, there was now a gigantic statue of stone, every detail of the ferocious beast frozen in the pose it had last held.

A cry of fear rippled through the enemy army as it beheld the terrible sight. What had been a sure victory turned into a terrified rout, the amazed Wishworks Army pursuing the fleeing enemy with triumphant cheers. Their leader had spoken truly. Hope had indeed come when there seemed like none was left.

◎ ◎ ◎

Ben walked over to the glittering hammer that lay on the floor next to Thornblood's cane and picked it up. Feeling the eyes of the presidents following his every move, he approached Penelope who huddled, white-faced, in the corner of the room.

Pointing the Impeacher at Penelope, Ben spoke in a quiet voice that was soft, yet filled with authority. "Undo your wish to control Wishworks, Penelope." Ben's face softened as he studied his cousin, seeing the terror and hate that was eating her up inside.

"Don't be like Thornblood. I don't want to have to use this." Ben glanced meaningfully at the small gavel. Penelope kept her mouth clamped tightly shut.

Ben indicated the view of the Factory from the open window, pointing to the black haze of smoke that filled the sky, pouring from the wreckage of what once was the most beautiful city ever created.

"Come on, Penelope. Let's work together to fix this. I'm sure that I can talk Thom into giving you another chance."

Penelope shot Ben a look filled with hate, and in that split second Ben could see that she was not defeated. He could tell that her resentment for him had been driven to a deeper, more vengeful place than ever before. But after a quick, horrified glance at the crowd of ghostly presidents waiting to dispense justice if Ben should call on the Impeacher's power, she turned back to Ben and gazed at the outstretched hammer he held.

"I, Penelope Piff, unwish my claim on the Wishworks Factory." She spoke through gritted teeth as if every word cost her dearly.

There was a gentle breeze and the presidents disappeared from view. As they faded, the light in the chamber rose once more, returning the presidential office back to its usual warm glow.

Ben lowered the Impeacher to his side and let out a relieved sigh. He had hoped his cousin would see the light, and she seemed to have finally come to her senses.

Ben said, "Let's go and see Thom. Everything will be all right . . ."

Suddenly there was a burst of sulfurous smoke and a blinding flash of light. Ben recoiled automatically as Paddy

O'Doyle appeared from nowhere, holding a pocket watch, and grabbed Penelope's arm.

The last thing Ben saw was his cousin's triumphant grin as she disappeared from view, leaving nothing behind but one of her pink hair ribbons fluttering to the ground.

Penelope Pauline Piff had escaped.

# CHAPTER THIRTY-THREE
## New Beginnings

*T*he smell of the freshly cut grass and lavender filled Ben's nose as he stood next to the gleaming marble monument that had been raised in Perkins's honor. Written on its surface was the simple yet profound statement, HOPE SPRINGS ETERNAL.

Candlewick and Ben stood silently next to each other for a long moment, neither of them able to think of adequate words to say.

After a long moment Candlewick spoke, breaking the silence. "You know, Perkins said something to me once a long time ago, long before you and I even met." He paused, remembering. "He told me that I shouldn't work so hard and should think about starting a family and having some kids of my own."

Candlewick stared up at the white clouds rolling slowly across the dazzling blue sky and didn't speak for a moment. Then, laying his hand on Ben's shoulder, he said, "I guess if I had been a little smarter and listened to his advice . . . well, what I'm trying to say is, if I had a son, I would want him to be just like you, Ben."

The words on Perkins's tomb grew blurry and indistinct, but Ben managed a smile as his eyes filled with tears. He didn't know what to say back to Candlewick, and didn't think that he could find his voice if he tried to, but he knew that Candlewick understood.

Candlewick gave Ben's shoulder a squeeze, then cleared his throat awkwardly, changing the subject. "It seems that Warren, Wallace, and Wimbledon picked up some intelligence. They managed to spy on one of the bands of Jinns without being spotted and discovered that the Jinns are searching for a way to recover the Lamp of One Thousand Nightmares."

Ben remembered hearing about what a terrible weapon the lamp was and how its evil power had been nearly unstoppable if it weren't for President Thicklepick and Cheeseweasle's inventions.

"So now that we have the Cornucopia and the Impeacher, they're searching for the other two secret weapons?"

"Yeah. No luck yet, though." Candlewick stooped and placed the yellow flower he had brought in the vase next to Perkins's grave marker. "I only knew about those two. The others are a mystery." He sighed. "We're going to need them. Although the Curseworks Army is temporarily defeated, I'm sure that in our weakened condition they're going to make another attack."

Candlewick turned his gaze to the Wishworks Factory walls. Ben followed his example and observed the crumbling ruin. Out of all the buildings, thankfully, the Thaumaturgic Cardioscope was relatively undamaged, and most of the wish-fulfilling equipment that had been modified to deliver curses had survived the war.

Ben sighed. The biggest problem now was the fact that the Factory had so little magic. It was only a matter of hours before the residual magic left from the Jinns was gone. Without their wish-fulfilling power, the Factory had no chance of ever being restored. It would be nothing more than an empty shell that would slowly crumble away.

As they walked back through the Wishworks gates,

they followed the winding lane that used to lead past the Feathered Funicula. Where the beautiful tower once stood was now nothing but a gaping hole. Candlewick had ordered Penelope's vulture cage to be taken away soon after her army's defeat. Ben noticed something on the ground and bent down to pick it up.

It was a single feather from one chair's mechanical wings.

Ben and Candlewick looked at the feather, each reading the other's thoughts. Out of all of the Factory's incredible machines, the Feathered Funicula and its flying chairs would be missed most.

As they turned to leave, a very deep voice spoke from somewhere behind them. Startled, Ben and Candlewick turned to see the last person that they ever expected.

Hoccus, the ancient Jinn, hovered behind them. Ben noticed that his eyes twinkled merrily at their shocked expressions. After a moment he spoke, breaking the stunned silence. "This machine of yours, it was designed by Bubbdouble many years ago?"

Candlewick answered, addressing the ancient Jinn in a very respectful tone. "Yes, sir, it was. Unfortunately, nobody knows where the plans were kept."

Hoccus nodded thoughtfully before reaching a hand into

the air next to him and wiggling his fingers as if he were searching for something. Then he pulled a very old-looking piece of parchment out of thin air, with a satisfied expression on his face.

"I knew that Cornelius had asked me to keep it somewhere for him, but I'm afraid that it has been a long time, and I had forgotten where I kept it."

Intricate, pale sketches done in brown ink covered the ancient parchment. Ben recognized the familiar design of the machine and its winged chairs. Candlewick studied the plans for a long moment before replying. When he turned back to Hoccus, he was grinning.

"I can't thank you enough for this." He glanced back at the plans, overcome with joy. "Your gift has helped us more than you know."

The Jinn smiled back and nodded. "I have decided to stay and help you for awhile. The boy said some things that made me change my mind." Hoccus glanced over at Ben, who suddenly felt an uncomfortable heat rise to his cheeks. "You have chosen your wish department manager well, Thomas Candlewick."

Candlewick chuckled and glanced at Ben in a proud, fatherly way, then tousled his hair, almost knocking off Ben's stovepipe hat.

"I wouldn't trade him for the world."

# ≋ EPILOGUE ≋

**D**eep in the bowels of the Curseworks Factory, Rottenjaw and Paddy O'Doyle watched as Penelope Pauline Piff, using a very elegant diamond-studded pen, added her name to the long list of the Curseworks presidents that preceded her. When she finished scratching her name into the massive tome with bloodred ink, she smirked and handed the pen back to the balding attorney, nursing her bandaged finger. Rottenjaw pocketed his favorite writing instrument and signaled for Paddy O'Doyle to open the doors.

A group of Spider Monkeys chattered excitedly as they marched into the room, followed by a procession of Horrible Snifters carrying a wrought iron crown on a velvet cushion. Bowing low in front of their queen, the long-nosed creatures presented the ornament to her outstretched fingers. Penelope regally lifted the crown, rested it lightly on her forehead, and then walked up the stone stairs and sat down in the black throne she would now occupy for many years to come.

Rottenjaw and Paddy O'Doyle clapped politely from the back of the gloomy chamber amidst the cheers of the monstrous assembly that whooped and clicked for their new queen. Paddy noticed that Rottenjaw held his usual quiet, calculating look on his masklike face, and they bowed low before Penelope before excusing themselves from the celebration. As the two exited through the iron door and proceeded to walk down a long, dank hallway, Paddy turned to ask Rottenjaw a question in a hoarse whisper.

"I just don't understand why you did it. She doesn't have any real *power* at all."

Rottenjaw's immaculate boots clipped on the flagstones and his dark cloak billowed out behind him, giving the impression that he was much larger than he actually was. When the balding attorney answered O'Doyle, he spoke in brusque tones that were as cold as the Curseworks Factory itself.

"Who has more power, Mr. O'Doyle? The one who *thinks* she possesses it, or the one who *chooses* to give it to her?"

The attorney approached a blank stretch of wall and produced a very thin metal key from his pocket. After searching with his fingers for an opening, he inserted the key and turned it, yielding a soft *click*.

A portion of the stone wall slid forward, revealing a dark hidden passageway beneath. Taking a torch from an iron sconce, Rottenjaw led the way down to a secret chamber filled with torture devices, surrounded by a wall of heavy oaken doors with small barred windows near the top.

The attorney walked to the nearest door, pushed the flickering torch near the bars, and peered inside. A low, pitiful wail filled with indescribable sadness emerged from inside the cell, and the attorney's masklike face showed emotion for the first time.

A big yellow-toothed smile stretched across Rottenjaw's face as he gazed at his prize.

"Come, Mr. O'Doyle. We have work to do."

# A Quick Guide to Conversational Jinnish

M'nud M'hari
(*MA-nood MA-hahree*)

*(Slang)* Usually used as a form of greeting. Rough translation: "I'm thankful for the Spirit that makes you breathe." *M'hari* is a shortened form of *M'hari shizbah*. *Hari shizbah* means "living spirit."

Jom'ba (*JAHM-bah*)

Good-bye. Literal translation: "We will see each other soon."

Mitha (*Meh-thah*)

Please.

Nud (*Nood*)

Thank you.

M'ka sharee
(*MA-ka shah-ree*)

"I would like . . ." For example: *M'ka sharee di z'shosi mitha.* (I would like two wishes, please.)

I t'bah de
(*EE TAH-bah day*)

"I work at . . ." For example: *I t'bah de Wishworks.* (I work at Wishworks.)

I sa'pak nu J'nnish          I don't speak Jinnish.
*(EE SAH-pahk new jeen-eesh)*

I h'naka raj t'bah           I hate homework.
*(EE HAH-nah-kah rahsh TAH-bah)*

I lavah zu                   I love you.
*(EE lah-vah zoo)*

Grob meh alla zu crishis     Give me all of your cookies.
*(Grahb may ah-lah zoo cree-shees)*